S·P·E·L·L·D·O·W·N

S-P-E-L-L-D-O-W-N

The Big-Time Dreams of a Small-Town Word Whiz

a novel by
Karon Luddy

ALADDIN MIX
NEW YORK   LONDON   TORONTO   SYDNEY

This book is a work of fiction. Any references to historical events, real people, or real locales are used fictitiously. Other names, characters, places, and incidents are the product of the author's imagination, and any resemblance to actual events or locales or persons, living or dead, is entirely coincidental.

ALADDIN MIX
Simon & Schuster Children's Publishing Division
1230 Avenue of the Americas, New York, NY 10020
Copyright © 2007 by Karon Luddy
All rights reserved, including the right of reproduction in whole or in part in any form.
ALADDIN PAPERBACKS, ALADDIN MIX, and related logo are
registered trademarks of Simon & Schuster, Inc.
Also available in a Simon & Schuster Books for Young Readers hardcover edition.
Designed by Einav Aviram
The text of this book was set in Bulmer.
Manufactured in the United States of America
First Aladdin MIX edition April 2008
2 4 6 8 10 9 7 5 3 1
The Library of Congress has cataloged the hardcover edition as follows:
Luddy, Karon.
Spelldown / Karon Luddy.—1st ed.
p. cm.
Summary: In 1969, the town of Red Clover, South Carolina, led by an enthusiastic new Latin teacher, supports thirteen-year-old Karlene as she wins her school spelling bee and strives for the National Bee, despite family problems and a growing desire for romance.
ISBN-13: 978-1-4169-1610-9 (hc)
ISBN-10: 1-4169-1610-5 (hc)
[1. Spelling bees—Fiction. 2. Family problems—Fiction. 3. Teachers—Fiction.
4. Alcoholism—Fiction. 5. Schools—Fiction.
6. South Carolina—History—20th century—Fiction.] I. Title.
PZ7.L9744Spe 2007
[Fic]—dc22
2006021956
ISBN-13: 978-1-4169-5452-1 (pbk)
ISBN-10: 1-4169-5452-X (pbk)

This book is dedicated to my mother,
Frances Robertson Gleaton,
for her extraordinary faith, beauty and strength.

To the memory of my father,
Cecil Lamar Gleaton—
the coolest man—Ever.

And to the memory of my sixth grade teacher,
Perry Gardner:
Her laughter nourishes me still.

Acknowledgments

With special thanks:

To my daughter Charlotte Bowman, my son David Luddy, and my soul-sister Sharon Wells Frazier for loving me unconditionally all these years—and for convincing me I had no other choice but to birth this fat sassy baby.

To my earliest readers for their enthusiastic feedback: my sisters Wanda and Sandra, Nichole Potts Gause, Rosalind Morrison, Henry Berne, Sally Miller, and Philip Loydpierson. To my Squaw Valley comrades: Melanie McDonald, Andrea Sanelli, and to Kim Whitehead for her superb editing skills. To Philip Cole, the Great Listener.

To my other true loves: Todd, Grayson & Genevieve Bowman, Erin Hubbs, Olivia Rozell, Margaret Currie Granger, Barbara Conrad, and Kenneth Smothers, my soul-brother on the Other Side. To my brothers, Brother, Jeffery, and Dennis, and all the other Gleaton family members. To Pat and Tom Luddy and the entire Luddy Clan.

To Talia Cohen, my courageous agent, and Alyssa Eisner, my crackerjack editor, for their wholehearted, painstaking efforts on my behalf.

To Fred Leebron for his literary generosity and to my other teachers and classmates in the MFA Creative Writing Program at Queens University, especially Michael Kobre, Jenny Matz, Pinckney Benedict, Elizabeth Stuckey-French, Daniel Mueller, Jenny Offill, and Cathy Smith Bowers, a.k.a. HomeGirl.

To Wayne Chapman, the editor of the *South Carolina*

Review, for publishing my first short story and for his unwavering support of my work. To M. Scott Douglass, the editor of *Main Street Rag*, for publishing my first poem.

To Pamela Eakins, for her brilliant book *Tarot of the Spirit*, which helped me fathom the intricacies of it All.

To my students and colleagues at UNC-Charlotte. To every person who encouraged me—you know who you are!

To every person who encouraged me while writing this novel—you know who you are!

And finally, to Tom Luddy—my brilliant and stalwart husband—for making our journey so comically *real*.

Of course I'm ambitious. What's wrong with that?
Otherwise you sleep all day.
—Ringo Starr

1

meg·a·lo·ma·nia

1: a mania for great or grandiose performance
2: a delusional mental disorder that is marked by
infantile feelings of personal omnipotence and grandeur

The sun bakes my doughy brain as I stand in the front yard, watching my twin brothers dance like little spastics wearing their homemade Indian headdresses. Bored to the point of madness, I fling my hands down on the brown grass and turn cartwheels all across the front yard, going faster and getting dizzier with each turn. My feet land in the flower bed, squashing one of Mama's Lilliputian zinnias that's full of tiny purple blossoms. I hold them to my nose. They smell like nothing at all.

I sit down on the front porch step, pick up a stick, and write *jackasses* in the red clay dust. This morning, when I called the twins jackasses, Mama accused me of cussing. She didn't care that *jackass* was in the dictionary. I had used the word in a cussy way, and that was that. That's why I won't be watching Gloria Jean ruin her life this afternoon. Instead, I'll be babysitting the twin male donkeys.

I smooth over *jackass* and continue to cuss in the dirt: *imbecile—maniac—moron—miscreant—bastard—doofus—* and *turdling*, a new word I learned at Vacation Bible School last month from Preacher Smoot's nephew, who was visiting from Miami. When the teacher heard him say it, she almost strangled to death on lime Kool-Aid.

I write some difficult spelling words in the dust: *serendipitous—myogenic—existential—*and *monosyllabic*, a five-syllable word that means having one syllable! Then I wipe it away and write *gargantuan*. I love that word. Etymologically, it's based on a giant named Gargantua, who loved to eat and drink and be merry. Since Mama bought the encyclopedias with the two-volume dictionary at the beginning of summer, I've been studying the dictionary like a megalomaniac.

I wipe away *gargantuan* and scribble *crapulous*, a word I discovered yesterday. At first I thought it had something to do with feces, but it comes from the Latin word *crapula*, which means intoxicated. I rub out *crapulous* and write *panacea*—a fancy word for cure-all. It's the word I missed last year at the Shirley County Spelldown. I'd never seen the damn word. Spelled it *p-a-n-a-c-i-a*. The year before that, I misspelled *ravine*, a dumb-ass word for gully. I spelled it just like it sounded: *r-a-v-e-n-e*, not *r-a-v-i-n-e*. That's two years in a row I've been defeated by *i*'s and *e*'s impersonating each other.

I go into the living room and plop down on the brown vinyl sofa, trying not to look at my sister's beige American Tourister suitcase sitting in the corner, packed for her honeymoon trip to Gatlinburg, Tennessee. Gloria Jean keeps the suitcase locked as if its contents were top secret, but I know she hides the key in her jewelry box. Every night, after everyone is asleep, I unlock the suitcase and sniff through her dumb matrimony stuff. The most disturbing items are the white see-through nightie with matching see-through robe, the white satin high-heel slippers with yellow feathers, and a half dozen pair of expensive lace panties in pastel colors. It's discouraging. I always imagined Gloria Jean would get hauled off to Hollywood by a beauty scout, not marry an insurance adjuster from Shirley County. The idea of her traipsing around in her panties in front of Wendell Whetstone makes me feel like puking.

A new wall plaque hangs over the mantelpiece. Mama picked it out of the *S&H Green Stamps Ideabook of Distinguished Merchandise*. "Chevalier and Steed" is how it was listed in the catalogue, and it cost six and a half books of stamps. *Chevalier* is a fancy word for knight. The plume on his helmet is crimson, the armor a dull gray. The only thing I like about the plaque is that the horse appears to be galloping as if the knight is in a big hurry to do something good, unlike Wendell Whetstone, whose main goal is to chisel my big sister out of my life.

Suddenly, without knocking, the black-haired, short-as-a-leprechaun, Snidely Whiplash–looking groom opens the screen door and steps into the room. His shiny black shoes crunch on the tiny pieces of gravel I was supposed to have swept up before company came. The fact that Gloria Jean might have to stare at his stupid face till death does them part makes me want to yank out my hair. Today isn't the first time he's come into the house without knocking. He hasn't even brought any flowers.

Daddy walks into the room, looking like a movie star in his navy blue suit. Mama follows, wearing her bad-mood dress, a beige shift that looks like it has tiny black daggers all over it. Daddy shakes Wendell's hand real hard while Mama fusses with the bent Venetian blinds. She's flabbergasted that Gloria Jean is getting married at the magistrate's office instead of Red Clover Second Baptist, but that's what Wendell wanted, because he was raised by a mama who is halfway convinced there is no God.

Mama walks over and pats me on the head. "Karlene, be a good girl and get that ironing done, okay?"

"Yes ma'am," I say, but feel like barking.

Suddenly, the bride-to-be steps into the living room, her red, wavy hair flowing around her shoulders. Gloria Jean's eyes are sometimes green and sometimes brown, but today I can't tell what color they are because she's staring at the floor. Wendell walks over and puts his arm around her and whispers something in her ear. She's wearing the blue linen suit I helped her pick out in the fancy-clothes department at Belk Department Store. That's where Gloria Jean buys all her clothes since she graduated last year and started working at Catawba Insurance Company, which is where she met El Creepo.

Gloria Jean walks over and stands quietly in front of me, but I can't look up. I rock back and forth hugging my knees, remembering how she looked the night of her senior prom, in that blue satin strapless dress, her long white gloves, and that tiny waist. The thought of losing all that beauty mutilates my nerves.

"Come on, Karly, give me a kiss for good luck." She lifts my face, holds it between her soft hands, and kisses me on the nose. The smell of Tabu reminds me of every orange I've ever eaten and every cedar tree I've ever smelled.

"Gloria Jean, are you ready to go?" Wendell takes her arm and pulls her toward the front door.

Daddy walks over and taps Wendell on the shoulder. "Excuse me, son, I need to talk with my daughter." Wendell steps aside and Daddy places his hands on Gloria Jean's shoulders. "You look beautiful," he says, like he's all choked up, then nods toward the groom. "Are you sure you love this man enough to marry him?"

My sister takes a deep breath and lets out a long, dull sigh as if she's been pondering that question for two hundred years.

"It's kind of late to be asking, if you ask me," I say.

Mama gives me a double shot of the evil eye, but I flip my hair. Ever since Gloria Jean got engaged last month, Daddy hasn't had a drop to drink, but I know better than to get my hopes activated. Any day now, he's liable to land up in Drunk City again.

"Yes sir, I believe I love him enough," she says.

"Well then, I hope you'll be happy." Daddy steps aside.

I can't believe this is happening.

Wendell shakes Daddy's hand. "I'll take good care of

her, Mr. Bridges, I promise." He escorts Gloria Jean out the door.

Daddy walks over to me. "Hey, Chipmunk, here's some M&M's for you and the boys."

Speechless, I stuff the packs of candy into the pockets of my raggedy cutoffs. My parents' shoes crunch on gravel as they cross the threshold and the screen door slams behind them. I trudge into the kitchen, open the refrigerator, and drink some dill pickle juice from the jar. It's delicious—cold and sour. Then I grab the broom and go to the living room and sweep the stupid dirt out onto the front porch and then onto the ground. Both of their cars are gone. Noah races up and down the driveway, pulling Josh in their rickety red wagon.

I climb into the porch swing. My feet feel itchy. My arms feel wingy. I'm thirteen and a half years old—my heart aches for some damn freedom! When Jesus turned twelve, he just went lickety-split to the synagogue without asking permission. When his parents finally found him studying with his elders, Jesus acted a little haughty, as if they should have known he had to be about his father's business. Poor Joseph probably felt like a loser, pretending to be Jesus' father all those years, but I admire how Jesus stepped out on his own like that at such a young age. It's ridiculous to think I could have as much freedom as the Lord, but that's exactly what I intend to get. God knows I'd rather be tumbling down Niagara Falls in a big, stinking barrel than stuck in Red Clover for the rest of my damn life.

The dumb ironing can wait. I need to study the "Dd" chapter.

Last night, while studying in bed, I came upon the word *death,* and a vision popped into my head of me and Gloria Jean sleeping in a double coffin. That's when I realized that we would never sleep in the same bed ever again. Gloria Jean was asleep, so I snuggled up close to her and hummed "Kumbaya" to myself until I fell asleep.

I grab the *A-K* volume from the floor and turn to the bookmark. *Death* with a capital *D* has its own separate entry: *the Power that destroys Life, often represented as a skeleton with a scythe.* Here's an interesting one about a *death angel* named Azrael who is forever writing names in the Book of Life and erasing them. Sounds like a punishing kind of job to me. Enough of death. I skim a few pages until I get to *debauchery,* which means excessive indulgence in sensual pleasure.

"Kaw—leen!" Josh screams. Then Noah. "Kaw—leen!"

If they don't learn to pronounce Karlene soon, I'm going to chew their big freckled heads off their skinny necks. I ignore their screams and keep plowing through the dictionary until I come upon two entries that are synonyms for beheading. The first is *decapitate: to cut off one's head,* and the second is *decollate: to cut off one's neck,* which amounts to the same thing.

"Kaw—leen!" they scream in unison.

"Holy Mother of Jesus!" I hop off the porch and run to the backyard.

Josh is on the ground, curled into a ball, trying to protect himself. Noah is standing over him, his face streaked with tears, holding the hammer above his head with both hands. I wrestle the hammer away from him and he just stands there, trembling and crying like a nincompoop. There's no use for me to play referee—the fight has gone way too far. Joshua's what you call a womb-hogger. At birth he was two pounds heavier and three inches longer than Noah. So when Joshua tries to boss him around, Noah froths at the mouth with revenge for what happened *in utero*.

At this point, candy is the only cure. I pull a pack of M&M's from my pocket and dangle it in front of them. Noah quits sobbing and wipes his face with his T-shirt, and Josh jumps up. "You two better get along or ELSE." I run a pretend knife across my neck.

"We will, we will," they say.

"Cross your heart and hope to die?"

They cross their hearts and hope to die. "Go climb a tree and don't come down until I call you." I give them each a pack of candy and they run away, squealing like piglets.

I walk across the street to our mailbox. Inside is a crisp white envelope with my name and address written in fancy handwriting. The *K* is huge and has curls on all four ends. I tear it open. It's from a new teacher who's teaching a Latin class for advanced eighth graders this year. *Superintendent Calhoun has been very cooperative*, blah, blah, blah. *She looks forward to meeting me*, blah, blah, blah. *It's time Shirley County tackled the classics*, blah, blah, blah.

Enough of that scholarly stuff. It's Cinderella Time.

I walk to our bedroom to get the ironing board out of the closet. Gloria Jean's fancy collector doll is sitting on top of the big laundry basket, wearing her purple velvet gown and rhinestone tiara. When they got engaged, Wendell gave the doll to Gloria Jean. Her real name is Marguerite, but I christened her Princess Samantha, orphan daughter of Czar Humperdink. What the dumb-ass gift *means* is beyond me. The fact that Gloria Jean gave up her dream of going to Bauder Fashion College in Miama, Florida, to get married to a man who gave her a doll crucifies me.

My calves ache when I think about having to iron on my sister's matrimony day, but Mama's been in such a twitchy mood, I don't want to aggravate her into a migraine. I drag the ironing board onto the porch so I can keep an eye on the twins, and then get the iron and fill up the sprinkle bottle with water. I go back to the closet and bring Princess Samantha and the clothes basket outside.

Maybe some music will help. I turn on the radio, and, as usual, Mama has it tuned to WGCM, which stands for "World's Greatest Cotton Mill." I twirl the dial away from the hog-calling song to Big Ways 61 radio in Charlotte. Ringo's band is singing that song about that lucky girl with a ticket to ride somewhere or another. I sing along, yelling out, "I think I'm going to be sad—I think it's today, yeah!"

I pick up one of the rugged cotton wraparound skirts Mama wears to work. Might as well start with the hard stuff. The skirt is so stiff, I have to sprinkle it twice with the water bottle. Mama's a firm believer in starch. She starches almost everything, and then hangs it on the clothesline until it petrifies. I press down hard with the iron as Wilson Pickett sings in a hot, soulful voice, telling Mustang Sally she better slow that Mustang *dow—ow—ow—n*. If I had a Mustang, I'd ride it all over town too, fast as I damn well pleased.

After I iron two pair of Daddy's dungarees, I sprinkle down the yellow checkered tablecloth and spread it out flat on the ironing board. Smoochy Lips Jagger is singing that doomy song about how his mind paints everything black, even the red door of his heart. Then they play another Rolling Stones record. Mick sings, "Here it comes, here it comes"— warning a girl that her nineteenth nervous breakdown is right around the corner. Mick sounds like he hates the poor girl as much as he loves her, saying she wasn't brought up right. Then he teases her about how her mama owes a million dollars in taxes and her daddy is trying to perfect a formula for ceiling wax. The joke, I guess, is that ceilings don't need to be waxed. So damn funny, I forget to laugh.

Before I know it, I've ironed three of Mama's work skirts, the twins' yellow button-down shirts and navy blue pants, and four white pillowcases made out of scrap material from the mill. After Mama finished sewing them, she embroidered them with a blue rose and a *B* monogram.

The basket is almost empty. Princess Samantha's head is sticking out above the rim. Her big blue eyes are staring at me in a real evil way, and I get that drainy, hypnotized feeling I get before one of those damn visions comes into my head.

I close my eyes and see a girl writhing on an old, splintery cross. Her head is bowed, so I can't see her face, but she's wearing that yellow polka-dot bikini Mama wouldn't let me buy at the Fourth of July sale. That pale yellow color really shows off her gorgeous tan. She stops trying to wiggle her way off the cross and slowly lifts her head.

Holy moly. The girl is me.

Immediately, I'm transported to that cross. Nails tear at my flesh and thorns stab me in the temples. Drops of blood trickle down my Frankenstein forehead onto my cheeks. I stick out my tongue and lick them. They taste like rusty lemonade. For miles and miles, I can see everything. Tumbleweeds whisking across the desert. Cacti of all sizes and shapes. Thousands of snakes slithering across sizzling hot sand. And way in the distance, I see Gloria Jean in her blue linen suit tromping behind Wendell Whetstone up a giant sand dune.

All of a sudden, I feel a sharp pain in my side.

My eyes pop open and settle on Princess Samantha. I yank that little mesmerizer out of the clothes basket and sling her as hard as I can out into the front yard. She lands on her back with a thud and a crack.

There's only one piece of laundry left in the basket: Gloria Jean's pale lavender blouse with the Peter Pan collar. I smooth it out on the ironing board, sprinkle it lightly with water, and press the iron across the clean cotton fabric. One of my favorite dance songs is playing on the radio, the one about a girl named Sloopy letting her hair hang down. God, I wish I had a cool nickname like that. "Shake it, shake it, shake it," I sing along with the McCoys. Suddenly, I am Sloopy Bridges, a sexy California girl sizzling under the fiery sun, my butt swinging in a pale yellow bikini, driving the surfers wild.

2

par·a·gon

1: a model of excellence or perfection
2: a perfect embodiment of a concept

Thank you, wounded Jesus. The longest summer of my life is almost over. It's the first day of eighth grade and I'm sitting in my sixth-period classroom with seven other wonder students, waiting to meet our new Latin teacher. Alan Ryan Smith, the handsomest, tallest, and friendliest boy at Red Clover Junior High, sits two rows away, sketching something in his notebook. He looks over at me and flashes his heart-melting smile. I ignore him and flip my hair.

"Does anybody know anything about the new teacher?" I ask.

"I do," says Desi Sistare, a.k.a. Mr. World Book, as he files his nails. Desi is an extremely well-groomed reporter for the school newspaper, and he interviews a dullard of one kind or another every month, mostly teachers.

"So?" Andrea says.

"She got her master's degree last spring. Her husband is the plant manager at High Cotton Mills. She has two small children, a boy and a girl. That's all I know. I tried to get an interview with her last week, but she didn't have the time."

The moment the bell stops ringing, a woman appears in

the doorway wearing a white toga that hangs to right below her knees. She stands there looking at us, her head cocked, one eyebrow raised. Then her face breaks into a huge grin, her white teeth dazzling against scarlet lips. Her shoulder-length hair is black and glossy. She sashays into the room, wearing brown leather thongs on her cute, chubby feet. Her toenails are as red as her lips.

As she swirls in and out between our desks, she looks amused with herself. Then she stops at the front of the room. "Welcome to my world." She bows. "My name is Mrs. Harrison, and what I'm about to say is very important. A smart person would probably write it down."

Everybody scrambles around, looking for pencils and opening their spiral notebooks.

"I, Amanda Harrison, am an extraordinary individual who fully intends to transform each and every one of you knuckleheads into a scholar of Latin by the end of the year, no matter how much suffering it causes."

A few students giggle, but I'm in awe of this woman. Everyone hunches over, writing furiously. I write down *Amanda Harrison, extraordinary individual, transform, knuckleheads, scholar, Latin,* and *no matter how much suffering*, with spaces between them for the words I can't exactly remember.

After everyone finishes writing, we sit there staring at her round face.

She continues. "Listening is a fine art you'll have to learn this year," she says. "But since you're new at this, I'll repeat the Amanda Harrison Proclamation." And she repeats the sentence real slow, emphasizing *no matter how much suffering it causes*.

I go back and fill in the missing words, feeling happy to meet a teacher who knows exactly what she intends to do with me.

"Okay, now that you know who I am and what I'm up to, please introduce yourselves and tell me the most important thing I should know about you. And don't worry—I'm easy to impress. Who wants to go first?" She pulls out an unopened bag of jelly beans and cuts it across the top with a pair of scissors.

Desi raises his hand.

"No need to raise your hand in this class. Proceed."

"My name is Desi Sistare. I have a twin sister named Deidre and she drives me nuts."

"Desi and Deidre—sounds like a circus act!" Mrs. Harrison says, then tosses him a red jelly bean that hits him in the chest and bounces on the floor. "Here's another one." She flings an orange one, which he catches.

"I'm Becky Miller and I plan to be a lawyer one day."

"Well, bless your *habeas corpus*, Becky." A yellow jelly bean flies through the air and Becky catches it.

"Hi, my name is Andrea Williams and I play the French horn in the Red Clover Marching Band."

"Watch out for those drummers! Trust me, I married one." Mrs. Harrison walks over to Andrea's desk and shakes a few jelly beans into her upturned palm.

Tommy Baker says he plans to be a United States Marine.

Mrs. Harrison stands at attention and salutes. "*Semper fidelis*, son. *Semper fidelis*." Then she pours him a handful.

I'm usually the first one to speak up, but I'm nervous as a tick. Mrs. Harrison has a large personality like Preacher Smoot—loud and boisterous and certain about things. It's thrilling just to be around her, but I don't know what to say. Definitely nothing corny about my family or church.

All of a sudden, my mouth opens. "Hi, my name is Karlene Kaye Bridges. I'm an Aquarius and I plan to win the Shirley County Spelldown this year."

"Well, Karlene, bless your lucky stars. Let me know if you need a coach. Spelling is one of my predilections." She stops beside my desk. "What flavor do you like?"

"I prefer licorice."

"Me, too. You must be a freak!" She holds the bag open.

I pick out three black ones. "Thank you very much."

"How about the rest of you? Anyone else interested in winning the Shirley County Spelldown?"

Desi and Andrea raise their hands.

"Terrific! We can form a spelling squadron. If you're interested, I'll be your coach. Who's next?"

Alan the Beautiful introduces himself and says he plans to win a basketball or tennis scholarship to Clemson University.

"So, Mr. Smith, you are the ambitious type—I like that in a young man." She holds open the bag and he takes a few.

Peggy Greer says she's half Catawba Indian and wants to become a doctor.

"Well, Miss Greer, I'm half Martian," Mrs. Harrison

teases. "Latin will come in handy when you study medicine." Mrs. Harrison doles out more jelly beans, walks to the front of the room, and puts the candy in her desk drawer.

"Ladies and gentlemen, I'd like to introduce you to the abiding principle of this class." She picks up a piece of chalk and writes big block letters across the board, pronouncing the words as they appear:

> EXCELLENCE IS OUR ABIDING PRINCIPLE.
> IT IS A MATTER OF H-E-A-R-T.
> IT IS A MATTER OF H-A-B-I-T.

Then she writes *Cor ad cor loquitur* on the board. "Does anyone know what that means?"

"Can you give us a hint?" Desi asks. She walks up to him, places her right hand over her heart, then places it gently over his.

"Heart to heart," I yell out.

"That's close, Eager One." She underlines *loquitur*. "Heart *speaks* to heart. Now, please repeat after me. Heart speaks to heart."

"Heart speaks to heart," I proclaim. Some students look perplexed, as if they can't figure out what she's selling. I don't care what it is. I'm buying every breath of it. At least she's not stumbling over words or acting like she has a corncob stuck up her fanny.

"Please be seated," she says, then circles *HABIT* on the board. "Now, little dearies, all you have to do is acquire the

HABIT of excellence. There are four simple rules for doing this." She reads them as she writes them on the board:

1) Do everything to the best of your ability.
2) Be willing to try new things every day.
3) Amaze yourself.
4) Sapere aude—which means DARE TO BE WISE.

She strolls around the classroom, challenging us to become Daredevils in the Pursuit of Knowledge. She lifts each student's chin and looks them square in the eye, saying something to each of us about being a miracle. "You are not a mushroom—you are a human being. You are meant to be wise. You are a miracle. I am a miracle. We are all miracles. It's a scientific fact—you are unique. You are one of a kind. There never has been anyone like you. There never will be anyone like you." When she gets to me, she says, "You are an original."

Then Mrs. Harrison walks to the front of the class and starts talking about "the glory that was once Rome," throwing out Latin phrases like jelly beans—calling herself our *alma mater*—telling us we have a choice between an *annus horribilis* or an *annus mirabilis*. She writes *Vivat, crescat, floreat!* on the board—commanding us to live, grow, and flourish as though there were no other choice. She says that it's a privilege to be our teacher. She writes *lusus naturae* on the board and confesses that's what she is: a freak of nature! Andrea looks over at me and shrugs her shoulders, but her eyes are dazzled, as if she's been watching a trapeze artist fly from swing to swing.

Finally, Mrs. Harrison points to a Smokey the Bear sign with SOLUM POTESTIS PROHIBERE IGNES SILVARUM written along the bottom, and says, "Anybody know what this means?"

"Only you can prevent forest fires!" we all yell like first graders.

"Just like I thought. A pack of geniuses!"

"What about homework?" Desi asks.

"Your homework each night is to reflect upon your teacher's brilliance, study your notes, and go over the vocabulary words for the next day. Every Monday, you need to bring in a list of five Latin phrases that you find interesting. The phrases must come from two different sources. That will force you sly coyotes to crack open something besides your textbook. I've put some books on hold at the Shirley County Library for the semester."

After the bell rings, Mrs. Harrison stands at the door, challenging everyone to *Carpe diem!* as they leave. Most of the students seem enthralled by her, like me, but a few of them look scared or perplexed or both. I lag behind on purpose so I can speak to her if I muster up the courage. Mrs. Harrison is the precise opposite of Mrs. Helms, a.k.a. Madame Blah-blah-blah, who has the unique burden of teaching me history for the second year in a row.

"I enjoyed your class," I say when I reach the door.

"I enjoyed it too." She laughs.

"Mrs. Harrison, if you ever need a babysitter, I am the absolute best." I write my name and phone number on a piece of notebook paper and hand it to her before I lose my nerve.

"Thank you, Karlene. I'll keep that in mind. Hey, maybe we could all meet after school tomorrow and talk about the spelling bee."

"That would be terrific."

"And don't worry your clever little head. I am *not* contagious."

"Oh, yes, you are." The words come out in a chirpy voice I don't recognize.

"Well, well, well." A four-inch grin spreads across her face. "I'm tickled you noticed, Karlene. Real tickled."

3

bib·lio·the·ca

1: a collection of books

A few weeks later, on Saturday morning, I'm sitting at the kitchen table listening to the Lovin' Spoonful sing that song about believing in the magic in a young girl's heart and how music can free you up on the inside. It is a groovy song, but it's not making me feel free at all. I have too much studying to do. I take another gulp of Dixie Darling coffee and pick up my black marker and write the hardest *S* words I can think of on my "S" poster board: *sanctimonious, serendipity, scurrilous, scatological, subterranean, stridulous, schizophrenia, susurration, superannuate,* and *strabismus,* which is the fancy name for being cross-eyed. The phone rings and I run to the living room and pick it up.

"Hey, Karlene, this is Mrs. Harrison," she says in her zip-a-dee-doo-dah voice. "What are you doing?"

"I've been studying spelling words since four o'clock this morning."

"Why in Howdy Doody's name did you get up so early?"

"I kept having this crazy nightmare, so I finally got out of bed, percolated a pot of coffee, and pulled out the dictionary."

"Tell me about the dream."

"You really want to know?"

"I absolutely insist," she says in her pretend indignant voice.

"Okay. Okay, already. If you insist," I say in my pretend aggravated voice. "In the dream, I am a huge yellow bird flying over a shimmery green ocean. My wings stretch out so far I can't see where they end. There's not a speck of land in sight, so I have to keep on flying and flying and flying. My wings ache so bad, I know I am going to fall out of the sky," I say, feeling out of breath.

"You sound all jazzed up. How many cups of coffee have you had?"

"A couple," I say.

"Tell me the truth, Jelly Bean."

"I'm on my fourth."

"Bless your little pointed head! Pour that coffee down the sink and put that dictionary out of sight. You're studying too hard! That's what your bird dream means."

"But the school bee is next Friday!"

"You are more than ready for the bee, Karlene. Besides, the Spelling Squadron has practice every afternoon next week."

"But—"

"No buts, Karlene. I order you not to do any spelling today. You understand?

"Yes ma'am."

"Now that we have that settled—I need a babysitter next Saturday—are you available?"

"I'd love to babysit for you."

"Jack and I have to leave early on Saturday morning. Do you think you could spend the night on Friday?"

"I think it will be okay. I'll ask Mama when she comes home from work."

"That's fine. Just let me know Monday at school, okay?"

"Okay, Your Craziness," I say.

"Hey, that's your title, not mine!"

"Not anymore," I answer.

"Well, hardy-har-har," she laughs, and we hang up.

Holy moly. I grab the "R" and "S" poster boards filled with tricky spelling words and thumbtack them to the living room wall. I can't believe I'm going to babysit for Mrs. Harrison. I can't believe I told her about my crazy dreams. The thought of spending the night with the Harrisons makes me feel perky. I pick up the phone and call Royal Taxi.

Later, when Kelly pulls into the driveway in his shiny yellow Chevelle, I'm sitting in the porch swing. Before he can get out and open the door for me, I run and plop onto the front seat.

"Where to, Miss Karlene?"

"Could you please take me to Weave Room No. 9?"

"Sure," he says, backing out of the driveway.

There's a new elephant carving hanging from the rearview mirror. I rub my finger along the purple swirl in the cedar. "Mmm. Smells fresh. I love how you carved the toenails so distinct like that."

"Glad you like it."

Kelly swears his name is Kelly Kelley, but I think he made it up. Last year for school, I had to interview someone about their occupation, so I picked him. Before he started his taxi business, Kelly used to be Colonel High's chauffeur. He even used to go flying with the colonel in his plane. I guess that's why he's so comfortable being around white people. I love how intelligent he is and how confident he looks in those crisp white shirts he wears, and that antique pocket watch he keeps in his black vest. Kelly's taxi service used to be over on Beale Street, where the blacks have their own separate little town, but a few years ago, he moved it to South Main. At first there was quite a ruckus about it, but Kelly had lots of white friends from the AA program, and they supported him. I sure have learned a lot about alcoholism from him. Plus, he only charges fifty cents each way to take me anywhere I want to go in Red Clover, which is a bargain price for freedom.

"Your daddy came by with the boys this morning on his way to Sadie's Pond. Said you kicked him out of the house."

"I had to study my spelling, but with the twins running around, all I can think about is murder."

He grins at me. "Josh pulled the cork out of the cricket basket and they all got loose in the car."

"I told you they were incorrigible!"

"Spell that one for me, Miss K."

"*I-n-c-o-r-r-i-g-i-b-l-e*," I say as we cross the bridge on First Street and climb the steep hill that leads to the Red Clover Plant of High Cotton Mills. "Mind if I turn on the radio?"

"As long as you don't play any hillbilly music."

I turn the radio to WGIV in Charlotte, and Jackie Wilson's chirping away about how disappointment used to be his only friend, but now he's got a new lady whose love is lifting him higher and higher. Kelly's snapping his fingers to the beat.

Huddled together on both sides of the street are small wooden houses with peeling paint and torn screen doors and red clay front yards, where kids play, looking halfway angry. The road levels off as we come to the back of what claims to be the "Million Dollar Mill." The red-brick building looks like a giant dragon climbing the hill toward town. Smoke spirals from its nostrils, and it's surrounded by a barbed wire fence with big shiny fangs at the top.

Kelly parks and walks with me to the guard shack, where he introduces me to the tall skinny man with a silver crew cut. I follow the guard into Weave Room No. 9, which looks like a huge, steamy cave filled with gargantuan looms that make a terrible racket. I cover my ears so I can hear myself think. All the women wear ugly aprons with big pockets, and their hairnets look like thick spiderwebs. We walk for a while until he points to one of the looms. I see Mama and make my way between the noisy machines. When she sees me, she rushes over and says something, but it's so noisy, I can't understand her. She pulls a pad of paper and a pencil from her apron pocket and scrawls, *What's wrong?*

I write, *Everything is O.K. Do you mind if I go shopping at Belk?*

She wipes her forehead with a handkerchief, reads the note, and acts relieved, but then she looks embarrassed that

I've seen her working so hard in such an ugly place. She pulls her small handmade leather wallet from her apron pocket, takes out a twenty dollar bill and her Belk charge card, and hands them to me, then writes on the notepad: *Pay $15.00 on the account. Keep $5.00 for yourself.* I give her a quick hug and turn to leave, but she stops me, then scribbles on the pad: *Be Good*, and underlines *Good*. I smile and nod yes ma'am, then rush out of there as fast as my legs can take me, promising myself I will never work in any kind of noisy place.

Kelly asks how Mama was, then drives slowly down South Main. The line is five deep at Liberty Finance. A woman dressed in white go-go boots stands at the back, smoking a cigarette. The One-Hour Martinizing dry cleaners is hopping with people picking up their Sunday clothes at the counter and at the drive-thru window. Kelly lets me out in front of the Red Clover Library and hollers good morning to Miss Sophia, who's snipping marigolds by the front door. "And good morning to you," she says.

I skip up the red-brick steps. "Hey, Karlene, good to see you." She hands me the flowers. "Mind taking these inside for me?" Her fingernails are stained yellow from smoking cigarettes, but they're nice and pointy.

I open the door and a cool dose of air hits me in the face. Not a soul in sight. Sunlight bounces off the gleaming oak tables. I put the marigolds in the vase on Miss Sophia's desk, then fill it up at the water fountain. When Miss Sophia moved to Red Clover last year, she painted the walls a pale yellow, then hung nice framed pictures of Mark Twain, Emily

Dickinson, and William Shakespeare. She also hung a big sign above the circulation desk: YOU ARE WHAT YOU READ.

The first time I met her, she asked me which subjects I liked the most. When I told her mammals, medicine, philosophy, religion, literature, and the occult, she looked at me kind of funny, then wrote it on an index card with Karlene Kaye Bridges at the top.

Before I start browsing, I walk over to the giant dictionary sitting on the fancy mahogany book throne. On the wall above it, Miss Sophia's sign says:

PLEASE REMEMBER THIS DICTIONARY BELONGS TO EVERY CITIZEN OF SHIRLEY COUNTY, NOT JUST YOU. RULES OF USE:

WASH HANDS BEFORE USING.

1) TURN PAGES SLOWLY.

2) DO NOT BEND THE CORNERS TO MARK YOUR PLACE.

3) DO NOT PUT YOUR FINGERS ON THE WORDS.

4) IF SOMEONE IS WAITING TO USE THE DICTIONARY, DON'T BE A HOG—SHARE!

I close my eyes, flip randomly to a page, and put my finger on a word. The word is *infirmity*, which means sickness of the body or a flaw in a person's character. The next entry is *in flagrante delicto*, a Latin phrase. It means being caught red-handed in the act of committing a crime. I pull out an index card from my pocket and write it down.

Miss Sophia walks over, reaches across the circulation

desk, and grabs a thick volume. She hands it to me. "Since you're interested in philosophy, I thought you should begin with an American first—and Ralph Waldo Emerson is a good place to start." I open the royal blue cover and study the drawing of the author. He looks tired, but satisfied with himself.

"These essays aren't the easiest things to read, but they're worth it. I suggest you read 'Self-Reliance' first, then 'Compensation.' Then just read them in any order you like. You'll find some excellent vocabulary words that will help you practice for the Spelldown."

As I leaf through the book, Miss Sophia rattles on about the integrity of my mind and how, as a scholar, I need to study the work of important authors like Mr. Emerson, and that I should *never* take shortcuts by studying what a lesser thinker has to say about a lofty thinker's work.

I turn to the essay on friendship and read the first sentence to myself. *We have a great deal more kindness than is ever spoken.* I read it again. I like how kind the words sound, so I write them down. Then I go to the reference area to look at the Latin books Mrs. Harrison put on reserve for our class. I select one and sit at the table. It doesn't take long to find some humdinger phrases, and I write them on a fresh index card. My favorite one is *Noli me tangere*, which means, "Do not touch me." It's what Jesus told Mary Magdalene in the garden after he was resurrected.

"I need to get going," I say as I head to the door.

"Let me check that out first." Miss Sophia takes the

Emerson book, pulls out the card, and stamps the due date inside the back cover. "Guess who they asked to call out words at the Spelldown?"

"Yeehaw! Now I know I'll win," I tease her.

"I don't play favorites, Miss Bridges." She winks, then wags her finger.

I say good-bye, walk across the street, and go through the side door of Belk Department Store. Red and purple balloons float above the back-to-school specials, but as I walk toward the junior clothes department, I feel all drippy inside thinking about shopping without Mama's eagle eye. Before she met Daddy, she worked in a fancy clothing store in Charleston and had a fine wardrobe. She's very particular about clothes. Every year, we always do our back-to-school shopping at Belk, and I usually get three brand-new outfits. But I can make do with what I have a while longer. Mama already spent a hundred and fifteen dollars on the school clothes she ordered for the twins from the Sears catalogue.

Instead, I make my way to the fabric department. Over on the remnants table, a purple velvety fabric catches my eye. There's a yard and a quarter of it. Enough material for a vest and a headband, which is perfect for my home economics project. It only costs two dollars, so I pay for it with my own money. On the way out, I spot five bolts of madras on sale. It is all the rage out in California. The Beach Boys look groovy in their madras bermudas. Earlier this summer, the saleslady told me that madras is named after the town in India where they make it. The weird thing about madras is that it's designed to bleed on purpose, just like girls.

The credit department is upstairs, so I climb two steps at a time and go up to the sweet red-haired clerk. "Where's your mama today?"

"Oh, she's working." I pull out the twenty and slide it across the counter. "Will you put this against our account?"

"Your mama pays every week, just like a tithe," she says as she fills out the receipt.

"She's a meticulous woman, that's for sure," I say.

"Well, please tell her Flossie asked about her."

"I certainly will." I stuff the receipt into my pocket.

I walk next door to the Midway Theater, hoping that Billy Ray is working. The kiddie matinee is *Born Free*, which I saw a few years ago. I'll never forget Elsa, that poor lion cub whose mama got shot while trying to eat the game warden. I look through the glass door but don't see anyone. I bang on it a few times and wait. No one comes. The movie doesn't start for another hour.

The smell of cinnamon and sugar pulls me to the bakery half a block away. I love the newspaper and magazine articles that hang in pretty white frames along the bright yellow walls. The first one is from the newspaper *The State* back in 1942, when the bakery won top prize for its Peanut Brittle Cake at the state fair.

"Hello. May I help you?" Mr. Tobias, our famous baker, is icing a huge tray of buns.

"Yes, sir. I'll take a half dozen of those."

He opens a large white box and starts filling it. Mr. Tobias lives in Catawba Hills with the rest of the rich people, but he acts respectful to every linthead that comes through the door, even Daddy on his bad days. I figure Mr. Tobias might be one of those anonymous drinkers, since he lets them have the meetings in a private room upstairs. I walk along the display cases, looking at the fruit tarts, sticky buns, pound cakes, and lemon meringue pies with lots of toasted peaks. Over in the special-order department, there's a seven-layer wedding cake with a corny bride and groom standing on top.

"That will be $1.32." He hands me the buns and I pay him.

As I walk into Flower Power Record Store, Mayor Melton's grandson is standing at the counter, dressed in a spectacular tie-dyed T-shirt, with his red hair pulled back into a ponytail.

"Hey, Rocky, did you hear the good news?"

"I haven't heard any good news lately," he says, lighting a stick of incense.

"Ringo came back to the band!"

"Hell, he was only gone two weeks." Rocky rolls his eyes and then winks at me.

I go to the "Top 40" section. As I flip through Simon & Garfunkel and Marvin Gaye records, Johnny Cash's thundering voice is half talking, half singing about how he shot a man in Reno just to watch him die. He sounds like a tired old werewolf growling for mercy.

Someone taps me on the shoulder and I turn around.

"Hey, Karlene, was that you banging on the door?" Billy Ray says.

"Yeah, I figured you were popping popcorn for the kiddie show."

"I was up in the projection room. Did you want something?"

"Nah. I just thought I'd let you know how everybody's moaning about how bad they miss you at school," I say, instead of *I miss the hell out of eating lunch with you*, which is what we did every day last year when he was in ninth grade.

"Everybody misses me?" His eyes light up.

"Oh, you know—the usual morons," I say. The light vanishes from his pale green eyes. I feel crummy for acting so nonchalant, but my feelings are all mixed up about Billy Ray now that he's in tenth grade. We've known each other since we were little because our daddies are fishing buddies. I love him, but not exactly like a brother. Besides, he's a Pentecostal Christian, which makes him a little preachery at times.

"I saw Gloria Jean's picture in the paper. Guess she got married after all."

"It's not a subject I care to discuss, if you don't mind."

"Uh, okay, then. How about our camping trip next month—you talk your mama into coming?"

"I'm trying to, but she's resisting."

"How about the twins, are they coming?"

"Unless I find a molecular transporter and zap them to Pluto."

A sloppy grin spreads across his face. "Okay, Psycho, what record are you buying?"

"I'm not sure, probably this one by the Rascals, 'People Got to Be Free.'"

He waves "Hello, I Love You" in front of my face. "Whatever happened with your wild crush on Jim Morrison?"

"That was last month," I say, trying to change the subject of crushes. Billy Ray's acting real weird, like he's caught a flirting virus. Last year, when these puffy muffin-breasts popped out on my chest, Billy Ray got all discombobulated around me, but lately, he acts like he's grown accustomed to them. Probably because he's getting an eyeful of those tenth-, eleventh-, and twelfth-grade girls' boobs sticking out in tight sweaters.

"How about this Gary Puckett song?" He holds up another 45 and sings, "Young girl, get out of my mind—" I elbow him in his side to interrupt his rhapsodizing.

"I like it just fine, but I'm buying 'People Got to Be Free.'"

"I'll buy this one for you." He walks toward the checkout.

I run after him and tug at this shirt. "Why are you doing that?"

A kind smile flits across his face. "A new record always helps when you lose something as big as a sister," he says, then turns to pay.

I just stand there, looking at his back, wondering how he knows so damn much. Around most people, I feel sort of made-up, but Billy Ray makes me feel real as dirt.

He hands me "Young Girl" and says, "I need to run." He rushes to the door, but turns around and says, "Tell your mama I said hey."

***

A while later I'm stretched out on the sofa reading Mr. Emerson, trying to learn how to rely on myself better. I hear a car pull into the driveway and figure it's Daddy and the boys, so I put the book over my face and pretend to be asleep. Someone walks into the house and stands beside me.

"Trying to get some sleep around here without the Amazing Bridges Boys?" Gloria Jean removes the book. "Come on, you want to go to the Creamery?"

"No, I think I'd rather go get my tonsils removed."

"You're a fruity-cake, Karlene. A real fruity-cake."

At the Creamery, we order a super-duper banana split to share. As soon as we sit in our booth, she starts talking about Wendell this, Wendell that. Work this, work that. *Blah, blah, blah.* But I just sit back and enjoy the view. Gloria Jean's eyes are bright and her lips are a glossy peach color. "Is that new lipstick?"

"Yes. It's called Tangerine Dream." She pops one of the maraschino cherries into her mouth. Gloria Jean acts different now, as if she's excited and calm at the same time. Maybe it's the freedom of not having to be a big sister and a daughter every second of her life.

I lean across the booth and ask, "How is Snidely in the sex department?"

Her eyes open real wide and she shakes her glossy hair. "Now, Karlene Bridges, I don't believe that's any of your business."

"Ah, Gloria Jean, *pleeease* tell me. Do you like it?"

"Uh, I like *it* all right, I guess." She shrugs her shoulders. "The first five or six times was pretty rough, but it's gotten better, I think."

The *first* five or six times. Holy moly.

"Since you've been living with Snidely for a while now, what's the weirdest thing you've found out about him?"

"Your brother-in-law's name is Wendell, not Snidely." She gives me Mama's lecturing look. "And the weirdest thing about him is that he irons my clothes."

"You're lying!"

"I'm telling you, that man *loves* to iron. Says it relaxes him. Every Sunday night, he pulls out the ironing board and irons while we watch television."

A vision of Wendell standing at the ironing board in boxer shorts flashes through my mind. I start screeching and scratching my underarms like a goofy monkey, then I stand and tip my imaginary hat. "Smart fellow, that Wendell Whetstone. Real smart fellow," I say, then go back to my monkey impersonation. Gloria Jean cackles, then yanks me by the arm and pulls me out of the Creamery into the parking lot, where we fall all over each other laughing our butts off. I have to cross my legs to keep from peeing on myself.

On the drive home, I try to talk her into spending the night, but she and Wendell have to take Itty-Bitty, his ancient, ratty little dog, to the veterinarian. Their marriage sounds boring as two graves.

4

per·snick·e·ty
1: fussy about small details
2: requiring great precision
3: FASTIDIOUS

"Desi, will you please spell *buccinator*?" Mrs. Helms, the Giver of Words, says into the microphone.

Desi sighs and clenches his fists. "May I have the definition, please?"

"A thin, flat muscle that forms the wall of the cheek, assisting in chewing and in blowing wind instruments," she says.

Desi grits his teeth, flexing his buccinators, the twangy odor of fear coming through his pores. It's Friday afternoon, the first week of October. Out of twenty contestants, only Andrea, Desi, and I remain in the Red Clover Junior High Spelling Bee. And I'm sweating like a piglet. Every time I fidget, my chair squeaks. There's a crowd of about a hundred seated on the bleachers. Mainly teachers, honor-roll students, and parents of the spellers.

"Mr. Sistare—will you please spell the word?" Madame Blah-blah-blah's acting all stoical, sitting at the table with the principal, but she's wearing a low-cut gray silk shirt that shows off her wrinkly cleavage. My sense of humor irritates the pee out of her.

"Yes ma'am." Desi pronounces the word, then spells *b-u-c-k-i-n-a-t-o-r.*

"I'm sorry, Desi, that is incorrect," Mrs. Helms says in her flat voice. At least we don't have to hear an obnoxious bell ring like we do at the county spelling bee.

Desi walks over, climbs the bleachers, and sits beside Mrs. Harrison.

"Now, will our final two contestants please stand for the final round?" Mrs. Helms says. We both stand up. "Andrea, will you please spell *buccinator?*"

Andrea smoothes out her red plaid skirt, pronounces the word, and spells *b-u-c-c-i-n-a-t-o-r.*

"That is correct, Andrea."

"Karlene, will you please spell *contumacious?*"

I know the definition, but want to stall. My eyes wander over to Daddy. He's sitting on the bottom row of the bleachers with his elbows on his knees and his face in his hands, as if he's watching a basketball game. He looks sober and handsome in his clean work clothes. "May I hear the definition, please?"

"Contumacious means stubbornly disobedient or rebellious."

In a clear voice, I say the word, then spell *c-o-n-t-u-m-a-c-i-o-u-s.*

"That is correct. Now, Andrea, will you please spell *hierarchy*?" Mrs. Helms pronounces it *high-ar-ky*.

Andrea makes a wimpy sound like a balloon going flat. "Will you say the word again, please?"

Mrs. Helms mispronounces it again. My heart skips a few beats for Andrea.

Andrea clears her throat. "May I have a definition, please?"

"It's an organization whose members are arranged in ranks according to power and seniority."

Andrea mispronounces it, then spells *h-i-g-h-a-r-c-h-y*.

"I'm sorry, Andrea, that's incorrect."

Andrea gives me a weak smile and walks away, pulling her kneesocks up along the way. I can't believe she didn't know that word. The Giver of Words ought to be able to pronounce the words, or else give up the job.

"Karlene, will . . ."

Mrs. Helms is talking, but I'm not paying attention. I breathe deeply, trying to oxygenate my sludgy blood, so that I can remember the contest rules about pronunciation. *The judges may not disqualify a speller for asking a question.*

"Excuse me, Mrs. Helms, but I'm concerned about that last word. Is it possible for you to check the pronunciation before we proceed?"

She gives me a double shot of the evil eye. "Pardon me?"

Not a soul in the gym moves. A sharp pain spirals through my temples. She's the only teacher I've ever had who I can't get close to, not even a little bit. I always try to show her respect like I've been taught, but sometimes it's difficult. She's pretty ignorant for a teacher.

I fire the second stone from my slingshot. "Ma'am, in my dictionary, *hierarchy* has four syllables, and it's pronounced *high-er-ar-ky.*"

Mrs. Helms's face looks like an old vase about to shatter. Mr. Barrineau whispers in her ear, then flips to the word in the dictionary, and they discuss it.

She rises from her chair. "Andrea, I beg your pardon, I mispronounced the word." She says in a higher, louder voice, "Will you please rejoin us?"

My blood is swishing through my arteries. Andrea comes up and stands beside me, and whispers thank you.

"Now, Andrea, will you please spell *dastardly*?"

"Dastardly. *D-a-s-t-a-r-d-l-y.* Dastardly," Andrea says.

"That is correct. Karlene, will you please spell *floriferous*?"

"Yes ma'am, I will! Floriferous. *F-l-o-r-i-f-e-r-o-u-s.* Floriferous." I enunciate every syllable.

"That is correct. Now, Andrea, will you please spell *gerenuk*?"

"May I have the definition?" she says, her voice shaky.

"A reddish brown antelope native to East Africa."

"Gerenuk. *G-e-r-i-n-u-k,*" Andrea says.

"I'm sorry, Andrea. That is incorrect."

"Karlene, will you please spell *gerenuk*?"

"Gerenuk. *G-e-r-e-n-u-k,*" I say.

"That's correct. Now, will you please spell *pluripotent*?"

I love this word. I breathe in and out, using the strategy Mrs. Harrison taught me, playing Hangman in my head. On the blackboard of my mind, I visualize the consonants first, leaving spaces for the vowels: *pl—r—p—t—nt*. Then I fill the blanks with vowels: *u—i—o—e*. The word is crystal clear on the board, so I pronounce it and spell *p-l-u-r-i-p-o-t-e-n-t*.

Mrs. Helms just stands there like an ice statue. The silence is deep and wide, as if time has stopped. But then Andrea starts clapping. Then Desi stands up and claps, and Mrs. Harrison lets out an earsplitting whistle as if I'd just scored the winning basket. The rest of the crowd starts to applaud, and Daddy raises his hands high above his head, clapping, clapping, clapping.

The principal says into the microphone, "Congratulations, Karlene. I'm proud of you and all the great spellers who competed today. I'd also like to thank Mrs. Helms and all the parents and teachers for their participation." He walks over to me and leans close. "It took a lot of courage to challenge that pronunciation."

"I felt it was the right thing to do, sir."

"Right or not, it was very brave," he says, with a look that says I'll probably suffer for it. Over at the table, Mrs. Helms gathers her things quickly, then slips out the side door. God Almighty. I didn't mean to embarrass her. Maybe if I kill her with kindness for a few weeks, things will work out.

Several of my friends and a few teachers come up and congratulate me. Daddy waits on the sidelines until everyone has left, and then comes over and puts his arm around my shoulder. "You done good, baby."

"Thanks." I stand there with his arm around me, feeling awkward. He's never gotten off work to come to any of my extracurricular activities before. "Why aren't you at work?"

"I told them I'd be late today because of your spelling bee."

Mrs. Harrison walks over and congratulates me, then offers Daddy her hand. "You must be Mr. Bridges. I'm Mrs. Harrison."

Daddy shakes her hand gently. "Mrs. Harrison, it's nice to meet you. Karlene talks about you all the time." Then he says to me, "You need me to take you home before I go to work?"

"I'm spending the night at the Harrisons'. I'm going to babysit tomorrow."

"Oh, I forgot about that." He squeezes my hand. "Don't forget to call your mama." He walks away like *Father Knows Best* in dungarees.

5

mu·nif·i·cent

1: very liberal in giving or bestowing: LAVISH
2: characterized by great liberality or generosity

"I need to stop by my husband's office," Mrs. Harrison says as her shiny aquamarine station wagon glides over the railroad tracks in front of the mill. She parks in front of a building that looks like a fancy two-story lodge, and puts on some lipstick. "I want you to go inside with me."

We take the stairs to the second floor, then walk down the hall to a door with a gold plaque that says JACK HARRISON, PLANT MANAGER.

"Good afternoon, Mrs. Harrison," a young woman says, then comes over to us from behind her desk. She looks like Miss Sweden from the Miss Universe pageant, her blond hair swept into a French twist.

"Please, Jessica, call me Amanda. I'd like for you to meet one of my finest students, Karlene Bridges."

I shake Jessica's hand. "Pleased to meet you, ma'am."

"Pleased to meet you, Karlene."

"Is Jack in?"

"I'll let him know you're here." She sits down at her desk, pushes a button, and tells Mr. Harrison his wife is here to see him. "Tell her to come in," we hear him say.

"Karlene, I need to speak with Jack in private first, then I'll introduce you two." She glides into his office in her flowing lilac skirt, white lace shell, and beige flats.

"Mind if I look around?" I ask Miss Sweden.

"Go right ahead."

Photos in dark wooden frames cover three of the walls. I walk along and read the date and description beneath each one. *1895*: the exterior of the Red Clover Plant. *1918*: Colonel High standing with workers in the spindle room. *1929*: spooling-room workers wearing uniforms made from company cloth. *1931*: the new heir to High Cotton, his shirtsleeves rolled up, standing behind a huge machine and looking cocky as all get-out. *1944*: a banner outside the mill proclaiming the Army-Navy Excellence Award. *1945–1959*: full-color ads from a campaign *that revolutionized the ad industry with its sassy, clever humor*. All the women illustrated in the advertisements have lots of curves and plenty of cleavage, as if they're bursting at their seams for love.

The last one is from 1962. It's a group of loom fixers standing beside the first Draper shuttleless loom delivered to the mill. I look closely and see that one of the men is Daddy! His head is tilted, and he looks young and wistful. Looking at these photographs gives me that sad feeling I get when Mama talks about picking cotton until her hands bled when she was little.

Miss Sweden types away, her long slender fingers dancing over the keyboard. If I could type like that, I'd be happy as hell. When she pulls the letter from the typewriter, I ask to use the phone. Then I call Mama and give her all the details about my victory, except for the part where I corrected Mrs. Helms. She'd worry up a migraine over that one. So I tell her that I'm in Mr. Harrison's office, looking at old pictures, and that there's one with Daddy in it. "That's nice," she says. I tell her I'll see her tomorrow. "Be good," she says, and hangs up. A lonely feeling arises in my heart, but I will it away, because I don't want to worry about Mama. Not tonight.

A while later Mrs. Harrison comes out of the office holding hands with Mr. Harrison, both of them looking flushed, but relaxed. "Jack, I'd like for you to meet Karlene Bridges, the new spelling champion of Red Clover Junior High School."

"Hello, Mr. Harrison," I say, and curtsy like the choir director taught me to do after singing a solo. I can't believe how handsome he is. Dark-brown hair. Clean shaven. He looks famous, with that crisp white shirt, fancy gold cufflinks, and royal blue tie.

Mrs. Harrison looks tickled about something. "Curtsying is only required before royalty." She laughs.

But Mr. Harrison clicks his heels, then bows from the waist. "I'm delighted to meet you, Karlene. Congratulations on your big victory." He motions me toward his door. "Would you like to take a look around?"

"Thank you, sir." I walk into an office that's five times bigger than our living room and ten times as fancy.

"I'll leave you two alone for a minute. I have to call Mrs. Cora, to check on the kids." Mrs. Harrison walks away.

"Wow!" I walk over to the aquarium that covers the length of one of the walls. Fishes of all sizes, colors, and shapes swim around in the sparkling clear water. "It's lovely, Mr. Harrison."

"I'm glad you like it," he says. "It helps relieve stress around here."

We walk from one end of the aquarium to the other. He points out various fish and tells me about them. A couple of bright orange fish catch my eye. "What kind of fish are these?"

"They are swordtails. The one with the long pointed fin is the male. An interesting thing about swordtails is that they all start as females. Some of them develop into males at an early age and remain small and slender. Some go through the full female stage and then turn into males much later. They're larger and thickset, like this one." He points to the larger fish with the sword tail. "And see, here's a female that remained a female." He points to a fish with a regular tail. "Notice how she doesn't have the fancy sword."

I stare at the fishes, thinking about weird fish facts for a while, and then I ask Mr. Harrison, "Well, since they *all* start out as females *without* the sword fin, and only some of them turn into males *with* sword tails, why did they name them sword tails as if they *all* had sword tails?"

"Uh, I don't know—that's a very good question."

"It's probably because the ichthyologist who named them was a man," I say.

Mr. Harrison cocks his head and wrinkles up his forehead

like he's impressed with my vocabulary. "That sounds reasonable to me," he says, taking a slender box of fish food from the shelf underneath. He hands it to me. "It's feeding time. Just sprinkle a small amount."

The aquarium is taller than I am, so I lift my arm and sprinkle a little bit into the tank, then move along slowly, sprinkling as I go, until I reach the other end. All the fish swim to the top and start gulping the shiny gold flakes. I hand the container back to Mr. Harrison. I like him very, very much.

The phone buzzes. "Excuse me for a minute, Karlene."

I walk over to the tall window that has fancy gold drapes pulled to the side. I stare at the gargantuan mill, wondering how many red bricks it took to build it. I can't get my bearings straight, but I think Weave Room No. 9 is on the other side of the mill. A vision of Mama's face flashes in my mind from the day I visited her at work. "Now, where were we?" Mr. Harrison walks up beside me.

"Do you have a minute? I'd like to talk with you about something."

He looks curious. "Fire away."

"A couple of months ago, the weavers had to start working six days a week, and it's causing some difficulties at home."

"What kind of difficulties?"

"Well, sir, since my mother only has Sundays off, she doesn't have time to be with me and my little brothers, or shop for groceries, or get her hair done. She barely has time to do any cooking or laundry. The overtime pay helps a lot, but I was wondering if there's a way Mama could have every other Saturday off. I worry about her being wound up all the time. The nerve situation in our family has always been kind of shaky."

He looks at me with a calm, serious expression on his face. "I'm sorry that it's creating a hardship for your family. I'll look into it, but I can't promise you anything."

"Thank you, Mr. Harrison, and please, please don't mention this to my mother. She would be mortified."

He reaches for my hands and holds them in his own. His palms feel nice and smooth. "Not a word, I promise."

Mrs. Harrison waltzes back into the room. "We need to get going, Jelly Bean. Mrs. Cora's having a fit with the kids."

Mr. Harrison gives her a peck on the cheek. "I'll be home by seven."

As we leave, Miss Sweden tells us to have a good weekend. She seems nice and efficient, but I sure wouldn't want my husband to be around that much temptation every day.

6

The Harrisons and I are seated around the oval mahogany dining room table finishing up our meal of baked cod, green beans almondine, tossed salad, and homemade yeast rolls that Mrs. Cora prepared before she left. The sound track for *The Sound of Music* flows through the intercom speakers. It takes me back to the beginning of the movie when that wild Maria soars up the mountain, spins round and round, and belts out in her astonishing voice about the hills being *alive*.

When the album gets to the part where Rolfe sings to Liesl in the gazebo, Mr. Harrison stands up, looks lovingly across the table at Mrs. Harrison, and starts singing about how her life is an empty page that men will want to write all over. And then Mrs. Harrison rises, acting like a young Liesl in love. She smiles sweetly and sings that she is sixteen going on seventeen, innocent as a rose. They swirl toward each other, dancing and blushing and sighing like teenagers. Mr. Harrison takes her into his arms and gives her a slow, gentle kiss. The kids, Celia and James, pay them no attention, but I'm tingling like a xylophone that's been struck a thousand times. Except on TV and at the movies, I've never seen humans kiss close up like that.

"Jiminy Cricket, it's seven thirty!" Mrs. Harrison says. "My bathtub is calling me."

"I'll clear the table." Mr. Harrison stacks our plates and takes them to the dishwasher.

"The food was delicious," I say. "Mrs. Cora sure knows how to cook."

"I'm glad you enjoyed it," Mrs. Harrison says.

"What's for dessert?" Celia says.

"The ambrosia's in the fridge, and you two need to help clean up."

"How can I help?" I ask.

"I forbid you to help," Mrs. Harrison says. "You need to bask in your victory. Go into the den, put on another record, and relax." She gives me a little hug. "You got that, Ace?"

When Mrs. Harrison tiptoes back into the den in silk pajamas, the dishwasher is running, ambrosia is in our tummies, and all four of us are playing Chinese checkers. "Okay, you two, it's time for bed." She stands beside us with her arms crossed. "Right, honey?" she says to Mr. Harrison.

"Yes, it is." He stands up and stretches. "Besides, Karlene is way ahead of the rest of us."

"No, no, no!" The children grab him around the legs and try to pull him to the floor, but he roars and swings his head from side to side until Celia and James squeal and turn him loose.

"All aboard the King of Narnia," Mr. Harrison says in a deep, gravelly voice. Then he drops to the floor and gets on all fours. Giggling, Celia hikes up her leg and tries to get on her daddy's back. James helps by pushing on her fanny, then he gets on and sits behind her.

"Good night, Lucy." Mrs. Harrison kisses Celia on the lips. "And you, too, Peter." She kisses James on the forehead.

Mr. Harrison roars, as if to say, "What about me?"

"My dear King Aslan, from the bottom of my heart, I thank you for taking these knuckleheads to Narnia all by yourself," she says, caressing his face.

He roars again and carries the children away.

By eleven o'clock, I'm stretched out on a fluffy bed in the Harrisons' guest room. I even have my own bathroom. The whole evening flew by like a perfect dream. My head is spinning from all the art books and children's books strewn all over the place, plus all those cool magazines I've never read before, like *Harper's, Vogue*, and the *Atlantic Monthly*. Celia and James are the happiest children I have ever met. I would be too if I lived in a gargantuan ranch house in Catawba Hills with a circular driveway, a two-car garage, wall-to-wall carpet, three bathrooms, volumes of leather-bound books, and a different colored phone in every room. And if my parents danced around the supper table, I'd pee in my pants with joy.

After the children went to sleep, I sat around the coffee

table with my pretend parents and sipped hot cider, then we stretched out on the Oriental rug and rested our heads on giant silky pillows. We talked and read for a while in front of the fire blazing in the stone fireplace. Mr. Harrison asked me intelligent questions about all kinds of things and listened to every word I said. When he asked me about books, I told him about Emerson's book of essays and how I had just finished studying "Compensation." He immediately closed his eyes and quoted the first line: "The wings of Time are black and white." I couldn't believe that he was a scholar, too. Then we had an uplifting discussion about the Transcendentalists, including Henry David Thoreau, Mr. Harrison's favorite, and my own personal favorite, Mr. Emerson. Then we listened to *Sgt. Pepper's Lonely Hearts Club Band*. I told them I adored Ringo because he was the funniest Beatle by a mile. Mr. Harrison loves Ringo too, because he used to be a drummer, but Mrs. Harrison likes John, because he's the most avant-garde.

One thing for sure, if I lived with the Harrisons, I'd get real smart, real fast.

7

re·gur·gi·ta·tion
1: an act of regurgitating
2: the casting up of incompletely digested food

Billy Ray and I are alone sitting on a hill near the Great Falls Bridge. In the past twenty minutes, he's given me a lifetime's worth of information about hydroelectric power.

"Five hundred acres of Catawba River out there in that reservoir," he says.

I squelch a yawn. "It's a mighty big dam."

"Yessirree, electricity is a miracle," he says. "God is so generous, he allows us to turn water into fire."

"Turning water into fire is pretty spectacular," I say, aggravated that the subject has veered to God, which seems to happen every time we're by ourselves. I'm glad I brought along my *L–Z* dictionary in case I got bored. I flip to the "Vv" chapter and scan the page until I find a righteous-sounding word. "Verily, verily, verily, I say unto you, Billy Ray Jenkins, doesn't the Bible get on your nerves sometimes—with all those *woe*s, *begat*s, and *verily*s on every page?"

"I like them just fine." Billy Ray shakes his head as if I'm an angel too dumb to fly.

"What about all those words with *-eth* suffixes, like killeth?" I ask.

"*Killeth* sounds like it might not hurt as much as killing," he says, trying to stop the smile about to break out on his face.

"Well, personally, I'm thrilleth we managed to ditcheth the twins back at the campsite so I didn't have to killeth them," I say.

His face crinkles up, and he laughs like he's charmed to death. Billy Ray's face is oval and his eyelashes are longer than mine. But lately he's grown as tall and muscular as a college boy. "When's the Shirley County Spelldown?" he says.

"Twenty-three and half days from now," I say.

"Hand me that dictionary—let's see if you're ready."

"No, wait." I pull out my homemade bookmark. "Let me ask you a question first!"

He leans over. "What's that?"

"It's a chart I made after I estimated the number of entries for each chapter in the dictionary. That way, I can figure out my study schedule better."

Billy Ray moves closer until his face is six inches from mine. "Don't you have any other hobbies besides spelling?" His pale green eyes look into mine, then settle on my lips.

"Don't you have any other hobbies besides Boy Scouts?" I look at the dictionary, but my heart's flipping around like a catfish that's just been caught.

He laughs. "Excuse me for asking!"

"Spelling is NOT a hobby, Billy Ray Jenkins. Spelling is the most important thing in my life. It keeps my brain working properly."

"Then why don't you pull a question out of that brain of yours and ask it?"

"Okay, genius, which chapter in the dictionary has the most words?"

Billy Ray pulls his little scouting notebook and pencil from his pocket. "Um, let me think." He turns to a fresh page and scribbles out the letters of the alphabet. After a few seconds, he circles *T* and shows it to me.

"That is utterly incorrect," I say, trying not to notice his pouty lips.

He looks at me kind of cocky and circles *B*.

"Wrong, wrong, wrong." A spicy scent of cologne zooms up my nose.

"Come on, give me a hint—is it a consonant or a vowel?"

God in heaven. I want to lick that smell right off of him. "It's a consonant."

He circles *R*.

"Another good guess, but it's dead-ass wrong."

Billy Ray raises his eyebrow like Mama when she hears a cuss word. Then he consults his list of possible letters and finally circles *S*.

"Correcto, retardo! And for your information, the 'Ss' chapter has twice as many words as the 'Aa' chapter."

"Come on, hand me the dictionary and I'll call out some words," he says.

"Not now." I put the dictionary on the ground and stand up. "Let's go to the bridge before the sun goes down." I figure putting a little distance between us might squelch the juicy Jezebel seething inside of me.

We wander up the hill into a patch of dried-up Queen Anne's lace. One of the flowers is as big as my head and crumbles when I touch it. Billy Ray walks over to the trunk of a giant pine tree and scrutinizes the bark. I wish he'd hurry up and earn that damn nature merit badge. I walk over to where he is and look around on the ground.

He turns to me. "Why do you always go around humming 'Kumbaya'?"

"What are you talking about? I'm not humming 'Kumbaya'!"

"Yes, you are. You hum it all the time."

"I do NOT," I say. But Billy Ray is not a liar.

"Maybe you're nervous about something."

"What do I have to be nervous about?"

"Spelling?"

"Oh, no, I'm not nervous about spelling. I'm nervous when I don't spell."

"Do you know what *kumbaya* means?" he asks.

"It's an African word, and it means 'come by here.'"

"As in 'Come by here, my Lord'?"

"Exactly," I say.

"I like it when you hum. I think it's cute," he says.

"Whatever you say, Billy Ray." I go back to looking around on the ground. "Kumbaya" swirls around in my larynx, but I don't let it come out. I wonder if I only do the stupid humming around him.

After a while, he says, "What you looking for?"

"Ain't nobody's bidness but my own," I say, determined to be mysterious.

"Come on, tell me. You looking for arrowheads?"

"No, Bark Boy, I am not looking for arrowheads."

He holds out his magnifying glass. "Maybe this will help you find whatever in the world you *are* looking for?"

"I'm looking for owl pellets."

"Do you mean owl droppings?"

"No, I mean owl pellets."

"What are owl pellets?"

I can't believe he doesn't know about them. "Owls eat their food whole and then cough up what can't be digested into a pellet that looks like a small stone." I say it like I'm an owl expert, even though I've never seen one in my whole life.

"Very interesting," he says.

"Come on, let's go to the bridge."

"You go ahead," he says. "I want to look around for a while."

I make my way up the hill and stand on the bridge. The reservoir looks like a huge topaz mirror. I love this place. Before Daddy's soul got trapped in a liquor bottle, we used to come here all the time. An image comes to me of a five-year-old girl standing in a blue wooden fishing boat, yelling and jerking on a small cane pole. Her daddy lays down his fishing rod, wraps his arms around her, and helps her land a big catfish. Then he gently removes the hook from the catfish's mouth and shows her the tricky fins. She touches the silky smooth skin. Her daddy lets the fish slide into the bucket with the other fish. The little girl looks up at her daddy, then at the fish swirling around in the bucket, thinking about how much that catfish loved the river. After all this time, I still feel that girl's heart thumpety-thumping inside of me.

"Hey, what you staring at?" Billy Ray appears out of nowhere.

"Damn, Billy Ray, don't sneak up on me like that."

He climbs onto the concrete ledge of the bridge, stands up, and looks out at the water, almost as if he's in a trance.

"Billy Ray, come on, let's go." He ignores me and throws his arms out wide, like he's enraptured with life. A cool breeze is blowing and the water in the reservoir has gotten choppy. Slowly, he turns around and holds his hand out to me. "Come on up."

I take his hand and scoot up the wall in my Converse sneakers until I'm standing beside him. Goose bumps pop out all over me. "It's scary up here."

He holds my hand tight. "There's nothing for YOU to be scared of," he says with conviction. We stand there looking up at the lavender sky, our hands absorbing each other's light.

After a while I manage to speak. "The sun looks like a giant egg yolk about to drop off the edge of the world."

"Yeah, it does." He squeezes my hand.

"Don't you love how dependable the sun is, how it shows up for work every morning, then disappears every evening like a happy servant in a hurry to get home?" Billy Ray doesn't say anything, just keeps his hand wrapped around mine. I sigh deep and long, then glance sideways in his direction, afraid to turn my head while standing on the ledge.

He glances sideways and our eyes meet. "You sure are in a poetical mood."

"It just gripes me how scientists say our sun is an ordinary star, like the hundred billion others in the galaxy. Because when I look at that ball of fire in the sky, I see God's Eye—and it's looking at you and me, Billy Ray. That Eye knows exactly where we are right *now*—standing on this bridge outside Red Clover, South Carolina—on the East Coast of the United States—on the continent of North America—on a planet named Earth." The silky stream of words floats out of my mouth and hangs in the air. We stand there holding hands, bedazzled by the sun.

When the sun disappears, Billy Ray hops from the ledge and holds out his arms. I slide into them and my head fits snugly under his chin. We stand that way, close, but not too close, listening to the Catawba gnawing on its red clay banks.

8

thau·ma·tur·gy

1: the performance of miracles or magic

As soon as we reach the campsite, Noah runs up and tugs on Billy Ray's pant leg. "We caught nine fishes and two of them had a bunch of little yellow eggs inside their bellies."

Then Josh yanks on my arm. "*Kaw-leen*, our tent is about to fall down. You have to fix it."

"Come on, I'll help you!" Billy Ray hoists Josh up to his shoulders and carries him toward the saggy tent. Noah skips alongside.

"Hey, Billy Ray!" Crawdad's sitting on the end of the picnic table with his feet on the bench. "Where in the hell you been?"

Billy Ray turns around. "At the reservoir, watching the sun go down."

"Well, ain't that sweet, Teeny? Preacher Boy's been watching the sunset," he says to Billy Ray's mama, who's sitting on our green metal Coleman cooler.

"Don't you start on him." Teeny gives Crawdad a hateful look.

"Leave the boy alone," Daddy says. A big lantern casts a golden glow on his face as he stands over by the picnic table frying fish in a cast-iron skillet on the camp stove.

"Hell, I'm just teasing." Crawdad shrugs his shoulders.

"Hey, Chipmunk, just in time to make the hushpuppies," Daddy says in his hunky-doriest voice, which means he's been drinking. My heart starts pumping like a motor that needs a couple quarts of oil. *Damn it all to hell.*

"I'll get the batter," I say, then walk over to the cooler where Teeny's sitting with a Schlitz in her hand and a giant bag of potato chips by her side. "Excuse me, Mrs. Jenkins. Mama put the hushpuppy batter in the cooler. I need to get it out, if you don't mind."

"Okay, sugar." She stands up and knocks the bag to the ground.

I bend to pick it up and she tries to help, but sloshes beer all over my back. "Shit, shit, shit!" she yells, and then grabs a handful of paper napkins and tries to wipe my shirt. She stinks of Lucky Strikes, spicy perfume, and Schlitz.

"Never mind, I'll go put on another one." I walk over to our tent as Billy Ray and the twins are coming out.

"What's that smell?" Billy Ray says.

"Your mama accidentally spilled beer on me."

"I'm sorry."

"Don't be. It's not your fault. I'm going to change shirts."

"Here." He hands me the flashlight. "I'll wait."

Later in the evening, I'm sitting beside the river in a droopy tent with a thin blanket wrapped around my shoulders, listening to a train whistling its going-someplace-else song.

The twins are curled up beside each other in a green plaid sleeping bag, their little bellies full of fish, probably dreaming the exact same dream. Just thinking about that kind of sharing makes me feel like Old Lonesome Me. I turn on our transistor radio, and from far away in Fort Wayne, Indiana, on station WOWO, an old song plays with no static at all—a song about finding a thrill on Blueberry Hill. I love the way *hill* and *thrill* and *you* and *true* rhyme. It's one of those tricky songs that tangle me up in the singer's feelings.

Cackling sounds come from over by the campfire. I scoot over on my knees and look out the window. The cackler is Billy Ray's mama, whose eyes look like watermelon seeds when she's drunk—tiny, black, slippery. I don't think she's one bit pretty anymore. Her biggest beauty defect is the half-inch gap between her two front teeth.

She's trying to get Crawdad to dance, but he's pushing her away.

Daddy's lying on a blanket by the campfire with his head resting on a log, crooning away. *Scooby-dooby-do, scoo-dooby-dooby, Scooby-dooby-do, scoo-dooby-dooby-doooooo. Strangers in the night.* . . . An image of the Harrisons and me stretched out in front of their fireplace flashes in my brain. I wish I could climb into that glorious picture right this minute.

I should have told Daddy that I didn't want to go camping. I knew he shouldn't be around alcohol. But I kept asking him about the trip every day. The reason I wanted to go on this trip is because I'm selfish. Sleeping in a tent by the Catawba with Billy Ray close by beats the hell out of being at home reading my Sunday school lesson.

Scooby-dooby-do, scoo-dooby-dooby-doooooo. Daddy's drunken voice shuffles the notes up real bad. When he's sober, his voice sounds famous. Daddy loves Frank Sinatra, Dean Martin, Rosemary Clooney, and Sammy Davis Jr. But Mama's crazy about country music. The way she talks about Loretta Lynn, you'd think they were best friends. I imagine Mama at home, wearing her lacy lavender nightgown, clipping her toenails, watching the *Porter Wagoner Show* in peace and quiet. Sometimes when I'm bored to a frazzle, I sit at her feet and watch that dumb hillbilly program, rubbing lotion on her smooth legs and bunioned feet. Jergens is my favorite smell in the whole world. Sometimes it smells like cherries, sometimes almonds. Mama knew better than to come camping with us. She can't abide Teeny and Crawdad being so trashy when they get drunk.

Scooby-dooby-do, scoo-dooby-dooby. Now Teeny's giggling and dancing all by herself, and Crawdad's over by the campfire eating flaming marshmallows. I look over toward Billy Ray's tent. Not a speck of light. I get my flashlight and crawl out and scoot through the weeds until I see three empty liquor bottles tossed aside. I pick one up and sniff it. Southern Comfort. Smells like orange juice and kerosene mixed together. Fried fish, hushpuppies, and Orange Crush churn inside my belly. I sit on a log by the campfire.

I look across the blazing campfire and see that Teeny has gotten Crawdad to dance with her. Mostly they're staggering around, holding each other up. Watching them makes me remember the Harrisons sashaying around the dinner table, singing love songs and kissing each other.

It's the liquor that makes all of them act like jackasses. Every time Daddy says or does something stupid or hateful, Mama says it's just the liquor talking. But when liquor gets inside of Daddy, it doesn't just talk; it sings, cries, stumbles, cusses, spends the house payment, and takes out loans at Liberty Finance without Mama's signature. Mama says you have to give the devil his due—that he always shows up when he smells weakness. Why can't the goddamn devil leave my daddy alone? The worst part is, I'm not even supposed to pray about it, because Mama says it's wrong to pray for anything specific. According to her, there are only four things I should say to God in my prayers: *I need you. Please forgive me. Show me the way. Thanks for everything.*

I belch once and taste the half-digested fish and hushpuppies. I belch again and a tiny bit of puke rises into my throat. I rest awhile with my head between my legs, listening to my heart beat. When I lift my head, Daddy's standing there looking at me, his face slack, his eyes empty. "What's wrong, Chipmu-unk?" His words are slurred.

"I'm not your goddamn chipmunk!" flies out of my mouth. Every cell in my body feels like firecrackers popping. I want to jump up and slap his stupid face, but I sit there breathing deeply, trying not to scream again.

"She's all right, Mr. Bridges," Billy Rays says, kneeling beside me. I look up into his calm eyes. He wipes my tears away with his bandana, then stands up. "How about you, Mr. Bridges? Are you okay?"

Daddy doesn't answer, just staggers toward his tent and crawls inside.

A while later I'm inside my tent, curled up beside Noah and Joshua, exhausted and numb to the bone, but every time my eyes close, I see myself yelling at my daddy. When I do things like that, it's like someone else is doing them and I'm just observing. It's like I'm *not the one* who bites my fingernails or pulls my hair out of the crown of my head—it's a tired little girl inside of me who's worn out from worrying about tomorrow and the next day and the day after that, and she's angry as hell.

To keep myself from feeling doomy, I start pondering miracles. Mama says I should never question them, but I need to know the particulars—like how in the world Jesus turned water into wine at that wedding at Canaan. I close my eyes and try to imagine the whole thing in my mind, but I can't get a picture to come into my head. Instead, I get this deep, rooty kind of feeling as if I'm a sycamore tree overlooking the wedding. There's a breeze blowing and birds chirping and brassy bells jingling. I stay in this tree trance for a while, until it dawns on me how Jesus turned water into wine. When no one was looking, he cut his finger and let a few drops of his blood fall into the big stone jugs that were already filled with water. It was a damn cinch.

Figuring it out gives me a victorious feeling, like spelling a difficult word. I've pondered that miracle for years—not only the wine part, but also why Jesus talked sassy-like to his mama that day, calling her *woman* instead of *Mother*. No one knows why he was snappy with her, not really. Preacher Smoot says Jesus wanted to let his mama know that he wasn't *merely* her son, and that he belonged to God. But I think Jesus might have been trying to make Mary understand that she wasn't *merely* his mother, that she was holy, that she could do miracles too if she set her mind to it—like turning water into wine at that wedding instead of him having to do EVERYTHING HIMSELF.

My brain gets a cramp trying to figure out what kind of mama Mary was or what kind of son Jesus was. No one will ever know besides them. Just like no one will ever know what kind of daughter I am or what kind of daddy I have.

9

du·plic·i·tous

1: marked by deliberate deceptiveness
2: pretending one set of feelings and acting under the influence of another

"God is the author of all our emotions," some preacher shouts on the radio. "No sirree—ain't no use whatsoever in running away from our feelings. God made them all. Joy. Sadness. Anger. Hate. Fear. Love. Disgust. Lust. Pity. Shame. Pride. And sooner or later, brothers and sisters, we have to face what's in our own hearts—the good, the bad, the beautiful, and the ugly."

Daddy's driving and smoking Camels like they're going out of style. I'm doodling jack-o'-lanterns in the margins of my Latin notebook.

"Mind if I have some of that water?" he asks.

I hand him my canteen and he puts it between his legs. Then he reaches into his pocket and takes out three BC powders and chokes them down with a swig of water. I feel an intsy bit sorry for him. His mama dying when he was three years old messed him up bad. I can't imagine being in this world without a mother. Mama's course is charted all the way to heaven, and she's expecting her kids to tag along right behind her, which beats tagging along behind Daddy into a piping hot eternity.

When I woke up this morning, three pitiful zombies were stumbling around like they'd spent the night in hell. Daddy looked as if he were trying to remember something and forget it at the same time. Teeny looked lost as a silly sheep, and Crawdad smelled like he'd just crawled out of the grave.

After Billy Ray cooked breakfast, we sat on the hill near the reservoir. He called out spelling words, but I couldn't concentrate. He kept asking me if I was all right. I finally broke down and told him how sick I was of living with Daddy. He sat there for a long time with his arm around my shoulder until I stopped crying. Then he talked about how we are not responsible for our parents' actions: "What they do is between them and their maker" were his exact words. When Billy Ray talks serious like that, I listen.

On the radio the preacher keeps exhorting about our emotions, but I'm too tired to *feel* a damn thing, so I turn off the radio and look over my Latin phrases for the week.

Errare humanum est. To err is human.

Memento mori. Remember you must die.

Ad augusta per angusta. To high places by narrow roads.

Cogitationis poenam nemo patitur. Nobody should be punished for his thoughts.

I really like the idea about not being punished for your thoughts. It must be a Catholic policy. Baptists believe that thinking something is the same as doing it. A phrase from Mr. Emerson's essay pops into my head, so I add it to the list: *Res nolunt diu male administrari.* Things refuse to be mismanaged long.

Finally, Daddy pulls into our driveway and Mama comes outside, looking refreshed in her church clothes—until she sees how miserable we look and how dirty everything is. Her mouth gets in that tight little *o*, and she tells Daddy he needs to stay home and bathe his nasty sons and put them to bed. But, Lord knows, I am raring to go. I scrub myself good and put on my navy blue jumper, white blouse, and navy blue loafers—clothes pleasing to Mama.

The Red Clover Second Baptist Church bus honks the horn out front. The bus looks pitiful, like a bunch of third graders painted it with white house paint. The wheezy old bus driver perks up when he sees Mama. He stands up and takes her by the hand and helps her up. I climb the steps by myself and follow Mama to the middle of the bus and sit beside her.

Three of the Ashley boys from over on the mill hill are sitting in the seats at the back, singing, "Ninety-nine bottles of beer on the wall, ninety-nine bottles of be-e-e-er, take one down, pass it around, ninety-eight bottles of beer . . ." But Mama keeps turning the pages of the *A-K* dictionary, calling out words at random. Easy words, like *amnesia, asinine, chronology, fiduciary, fumigate*, and *intravenous*. She's trying to act enthusiastic, but I can tell she knows Daddy jumped off the Sober Train again.

His drinking is not something she likes to talk about. Every time I bring it up, she acts like it's her own private problem. Mama acts like God's love is plenty enough to save him from his drunkenness, but I think it's going to take a whole lot more than that. When it comes to Daddy, it's as if she doesn't want to know the truth. Putting a finger on her feelings isn't one of Mama's strengths, but I think she's lonely as the moon.

Training Union bored me to pieces, but I've never felt so damn happy to walk into the Lord's house on baptism night. Mama and I take our usual seats on the fourth pew on the right side. There's something magical about how the light reflects off the baptismal waters tonight, flinging little Tinkerbells all over the sanctuary walls. I feel like running up to Preacher Smoot and telling him to give me a good dunking before he even starts his sermon—but I don't dare. Mama would be mortified. I've been baptized twice already, which, according to her, is one time too many.

So, instead, I close my eyes and remember the first time I was baptized. The water feels warm as a baby's bath, my crinoline is heavy with holy water, the yellow sash of my white dress streams behind me. Preacher Smoot places his gargantuan hand upon my head and turns me toward the congregation. Then he blesses me, lowers me into the water, and holds me under for what seems like a long time. Finally, he lifts me out of the water, and I stumble up the stairs out of the baptistery, sputtering water, about to choke on my own salvation.

10

es·ca·pade

1: an act of breaking loose from rules or restraint
2: an adventurous action that runs counter to approved
conduct

"Mr. Satterfield, will you please spell *causalgia*?" Miss Sophia says, standing behind the podium at the left of the stage.

"May I have the definition, please?" Jack squeaks into the microphone. Only five contestants remain. The other four of us are sitting in orange plastic chairs arranged in a semicircle on the stage.

"An intense, burning pain, usually neuralgic," Miss Sophia says. She's doing a great job as the Giver of Words, plus she looks snazzy in her new black tailored pantsuit with a white shirt and red scarf.

Jack rubs the back of his neck. "*C-a-u-s-a-l-g-e-a.*"

The bell rings. Poor Jack trudges down the steps into the auditorium and joins the other seventeen spellers who heard the fatal bell ring. Being a two-time loser myself, I feel sorry as hell for them, but deep inside I feel victorious. So far, I've had a couple of easy words: *vehicular* and *guerrilla*. The others were more difficult: *dyspeptic*, *étagère*, and *neurotic*, which is a fancy way of saying you have a bad case of the cooties inside your brain.

"Miss Harper, will you please spell *craniopagus*?"

Cherry Harper, the eighth grader who beat me last year, goes to the microphone. Her jet-black hair is wound into a messy French twist that looks like it's been shellacked. "May I have a definition, please?"

Miss Sophia says, "Craniopagus is a condition in which Siamese twins are born with their heads joined."

From out of nowhere a huge laugh wells up in my stomach. I try to squelch it by biting my tongue, but it shoots straight up my esophagus, and a noise comes out of me that sounds like a hee-hawing donkey. An image of Noah and Joshua joined at the top of their heads keeps flashing in my mind. I shut my eyes as tightly as I can, trying to squeeze the image out of my head, but the hee-hawing gets louder. A little bit of pee leaks into my panties. Oh, my God. I'm not going to be able to stop laughing. It's like all the nonsense inside of me is percolating to the outside, and I can barely see a damn thing for the tears pouring out of my eyes. Miss Sophia is standing in front of me with her hands on my shoulders, shushing me in a sweet voice. "Shh. It's going to be all right. Just breathe, Karlene, breathe. You need to get ahold of yourself."

I focus on her face and breathe deeply, trying to force the whole gob of laughter out of me all at once, but it comes out in shrieky spurts, then tapers off into a few hiccups before it vanishes. I close my eyes and sit there, breathing in and out. Miss Sophia hands me a tissue. There's not one snicker in the entire auditorium. The silence is so damn beautiful.

I open my eyes. Miss Sophia smiles and hands me a fresh tissue. "You okay now?"

I nod my head. The auditorium is still filled with absolute silence.

"Thank you. I'm ready to continue," I say, and then blow my nose real good.

Miss Sophia nods and walks back to the podium. "Pardon the interruption, Miss Harper. Now, will you please spell *craniopagus*?"

Not one syllable sounds funny to me. Hallelujah. Another miracle.

Cherry spells the word correctly, sits beside me, and gives me an encouraging pat on the back, acting dignified as a champion. Trent Thomas misspells *amoebocyte*, walks from the stage, and wanders right on out of the auditorium. Benny Gilroy offers a totally original combination of letters for *facetiously*, and acts relieved to hear the bell. He nearly skips from the stage, obviously unaware that *facetiously* is famous for being the shortest word that has all the vowels in order: Even the sometimes *y* is at the end.

Miss Sophia asks Cherry and me to stand up, and we battle it out, spelling *irrevocable, bhakti, fictioneering, gudgeon, jettison, chanteuse, smorgasbord, predilection, otitis, googolplex*. Finally, Cherry stumbles over *pinaceous*. Spells it *pinacious*. The bell rings, and Cherry drops her head and groans. Poor thing got foiled by those damn *e*'s and *i*'s.

"Miss ... Bridges ... will ... you ... please ... spell ... *pinaceous*?"

Everything has slowed way down. My temples throb from all the blood surging around in my brain. I can't feel my skin. Or my skin can't feel me. I feel as if I've vanished except for my eyes and brain. I keep myself from looking at the Harrisons, but I can't resist looking over at Mama, who's sitting proudly between Daddy and Kelly. I'm thrilled they're all here. Thrilled that Kelly is such a good sponsor and talked Daddy into going back to AA. *Damn.* I need to focus. I force myself to erase everything from my mind like Mrs. Harrison taught me.

"Will you please repeat the word, Miss Sophia?"

She repeats the word. It hangs in the air for a while.

I focus on the vibration of the word against my eardrums. Then I relax and let the letters make themselves into a word in my mind. Then I examine it and see if it feels right. It feels exactly right, so I spell it: "*P-i-n-a-c-e-o-u-s.*"

"That is correct, Miss Bridges." Miss Sophia's words come out at regular speed. Poor Cherry moans. I smell the salty scent of despair leaking from her pores.

"Now, will you please spell *her—easy—ark?*" Miss Sophia says.

It's a word I've never heard. My heart feels like a cartoon heart thumping right out of my chest. "May I have the definition, please?"

"It means the founder or leader of a heresy. Someone with unorthodox practices or beliefs."

Hmm. Heresy. Unorthodox practices or beliefs. I breathe deeply and think about Jesus as a Jewish boy studying in the synagogue. And then I think about when he grew up, how he stormed into the temple, popping a whip at the people who were selling oxen and sheep and doves to be slaughtered. He was pissed off about their defiling a holy place with their bloody business, so he overturned their tables and chased them out of the temple. I bet that's when the church leaders decided Jesus was a heretic and needed to be squelched.

Miss Sophia clears her throat twice.

I ask her to repeat the word.

She pronounces it again: *her—easy—ark*.

I see *heresy* in my mind. Then I see *monarch*. I put them side by side and let them melt together. I pronounce the word, and then say the letters that I see: "*H-e-r-e-s-i-a-r-c-h*."

Mrs. Harrison's earsplitting whistle tells me everything I need to know.

"Congratulations, Miss Bridges, you are the new Spelling Champion of Shirley County!" Miss Sophia says it like she's introducing a royal "heiness."

11

pre·rog·a·tive

1: an exclusive or special right, power, or privilege
2: a special superiority of right or privilege

"Jiminy Cricket, it's seven thirty! We need to be at the party in thirty minutes." Mrs. Harrison rises from the table. "Karlene, there's some sherbet in the fridge. And you two," she says to Celia and James, "you need to help clean up the kitchen."

"The food was delicious," I say.

"I'm glad you enjoyed it." Mrs. Harrison smiles and rushes from the table to get ready for the fancy Day-After-Thanksgiving gala at the mayor's house.

"I'll clear the table." Mr. Harrison picks up all the plates and silverware, but I stop him and tell him we'll do the rest. He says thanks and leaves to get dressed.

By the time the Harrisons come downstairs, the kitchen is spotless, and the kids and I are sprawled on the Oriental rug in the den, playing a game of Old Maid. Mrs. Harrison is wearing a pale blue backless dress; her healthy shoulders glow under a lace shawl. Mr. Harrison's tuxedo fits him perfectly. He is terribly handsome, but he has a sweet, dignified smile, like Kelly. He winks at me. "Okay, you two, promise me you'll be good for Karlene."

The children grab him around the legs, promising to be

good. Mrs. Harrison gives them a quick hug and writes down the phone number at the mayor's house for me. Then she puts her hands on my face and looks me in the eye. "Don't forget the ten-yard rule, Your Craziness."

Her hands feel soft as rose petals on my face, so I stall. "Whatever are you talking about, Your Saneness?"

"The rule that says if you get within ten yards of the dictionary, your tongue will be surgically removed."

"Oh, that silly rule."

She chuckles and walks out the kitchen door.

After building a fortress with Tinkertoys, we go to the guest room, which now belongs to me, because there's a white ceramic star on the door with KARLENE painted on it. Celia and James stretch out on the new white bedspread with lavender rosebuds embroidered on it and color another turkey in their Thanksgiving coloring books. I prop myself up on two fat pillows made out of the same silky fabric, and look at the art book full of paintings by Marc Chagall. Each painting is like a happy dream that's about to turn into a nightmare. They're full of upside-down choo-choo trains, animals floating sideways, mermaids playing violins, lovers with their faces melted together, and angels opening bedroom windows.

My favorite picture is called *I and the Village*. There's a profile view of a handsome, human-looking lamb wearing a necklace of multicolored beads talking to a green-faced man with white lips. Painted on the lamb's jaw is a goat with a bulging udder that's being milked by a woman in a green skirt, sitting on a stool. The village is in the background, perched on a hill. In the middle of the village, a woman is standing on her head, and a man is walking toward her carrying a pitchfork. The sky is painted in swirls of blue and red and green and pink. Two of the houses are upside down. There's a round church with a cross on top and a monster-size priest waiting at the door. All those images living in the same painting makes the village utterly wild, but it's nothing to snicker over, no matter how mixed up it seems to be.

By the time I put the book aside, it's almost midnight, and James and Celia are cuddled up beside me, sound asleep. I get up and go to the closet to look at the scarlet red coat Mrs. Harrison gave me today. She said she bought it for herself a couple years ago, but it smells brand-new. I put it on and stand in front of the full-length mirror in the hall, looking like Little Miss Riding Hood before she meets the wolf. I twirl around and around, hugging myself. The red satin lining of the hood feels sexy against my face. I hang the coat up and go into the sparkling white bathroom, wash my face, and then dry it with a fluffy purple towel, thinking how wonderful it would be to have a housekeeper like Mrs. Cora.

I whisper "I love you" into the mirror, and then kiss its cool, clean surface. I have never actually kissed anyone's lips, but in my imagination I've kissed hundreds of people: the cute new choir director at church; most of the stock boys at the Winn-Dixie; Ricky Worth, the Red Clover Tornadoes quarterback; and Billy Ray Jenkins. I pretend to kiss famous people all the time: Joe Namath, of the New York Jets; David Janssen, the poor Fugitive on TV; and, of course, Ringo, by far the most charismatic and kissable of the Fab Four. Sometimes I even pretend I am Mrs. Harrison kissing Mr. Harrison, and vice versa. Mrs. Harrison likes to nibble on Mr. Harrison's bottom lip, but Mr. Harrison likes to plunge his tongue into Mrs. Harrison's mouth after a long, smooth, silky kiss.

As I finish brushing my teeth, I see the Harrisons tiptoe by in the hall. They don't see me, so I follow them into my bedroom and help them pull the covers off the kids. Mr. Harrison picks up James, and Mrs. Harrison, Celia, and they carry them to their rooms. I get into bed and start looking at the art book again.

After a while I hear water filling their bathtub. I go back to my bathroom, sit on the toilet lid, and put my ear to the wall. Someone's gargling. Mrs. Harrison oohs and aahs as she lowers herself into the water. Now, they're talking. I picture Mr. Harrison sitting backward on the blue velvet vanity chair talking to his wife. Holy Mother, they're discussing me! I can't make out everything they say because she's splashing around in the water, but I can hear certain of Mr. Harrison's words. *Alcoholic. Loom fixer. Three needy children at home. Decent, hardworking mother.* Then Mrs. Harrison's saying things about *poor Karlene . . . Funny. Sweet. Brilliant. Lonely. Confused. Most ambitious child God ever made.* But Mrs. Harrison's voice has that same hand-wringing sound as Mama's and makes me feel like poor Eleanor Rigby picking up rice in a church where a wedding has been. I feel horrified by how tragic my story sounds coming from their lips. They quit talking for a while and I imagine Mr. Harrison washing her back with a fluffy bath cloth and lavender soap to soothe her. I close my eyes, listening to the silence, and think about how some words ought to be spelled with triple letters. Words like *terrrible* and *flabbbergasted* and *innnocent*.

Mrs. Harrison is talking again, so I listen closely. "No matter how smart she is, her dreams can only take her so far. Her home life is a mess. What if she loses the state spelling bee, Jack? What in God's name will she do?"

"She would come up with a new dream," Mr. Harrison says, "and we'd help her. Now come on, let's go to bed."

I stand up and look at the girl in the mirror, with droopy blue eyes and clenched jaws. What do the Harrisons know about the Bridges family, anyway? Nothing. Maybe Mr. Harrison has been nosying around the mill, asking the boss men about Mama and Daddy. But nobody really understands how hard Daddy's trying to be good. They don't know he hasn't had a drop to drink in four weeks. Mrs. Harrison is full of rotten baloney. Telling me *Sapere aude, sapere aude, sapere aude*. And I believed her—I am daring to be wise, I am studying my butt off—but, deep inside, she thinks I am *dooomed*. I don't need anybody's sympathy. I am the spelling champion of Shirley County. In January I will become the spelling champion of South Carolina. And then in May I'll march into Washington, D.C., and win the spelling championship of the United States of America. Who knows? I might even become the spelling champion of the whole goddamn world.

I trudge back to bed, but my heart feels restless and I flop around on the bed, biting my fingernails. An image of me and Billy Ray standing on the ledge of the bridge comes into my head, and I relax. The sun is pure gold. The breeze ruffles my hair. We're holding hands, admiring the sun sinking into the reservoir. I wonder how he really feels about me. What he thinks of me being so ornery and smart-alecky all the time. He talks like a prophet and never judges anyone, even though he has to live with two drunk parents. He's probably going to be a famous preacher like Billy Graham one day. It's silly to have these romantic thoughts about him, because it's obvious he's God's boy. But when it comes to Billy Ray Jenkins, my imagination gets diarrhea.

Mrs. Harrison knocks, and then comes in and sits on the bed. "Hey, champ," she says, gently pushing my bangs aside. The feel of her fingers on my forehead makes my anger float up to heaven. She tells me all about Mayor Melton's shindig and asks me about what we did and how the kids behaved. She notices the art book on the nightstand and starts talking about Marc Chagall this and Marc Chagall that. Then she plumps up a pillow beside me and we look at the village picture. "Look, it's a girl milking a billy goat! I wonder why he painted it there on the lamb's cheek?"

"I don't think that's a billy goat," I say.

"You don't?"

"No ma'am. Billy goats don't have udders," I say without cracking a smile.

She leans over and starts tickling me under my arms. I

break out in wild giggles and try to push her away. But she holds on and we tumble across the bed until we roll off and hit the soft green carpet. After we untangle ourselves, we lie there laughing our butts off. Finally, we settle down and I hop into bed.

She tucks me in and kisses my forehead. "Sweet dreams, Jelly Bean."

"Good night, Your Craziness," I say.

"Light off?" she says, her finger on the lamp switch.

"No, thanks. I want to look at a few more paintings."

She walks away, but the musky smell of her perfume lingers. I pick up the book and turn back to the magical village. There is something peculiar about the milkmaid. One of her hands appears to be tied behind her back.

12

dis·equi·lib·ri·um

1: loss of stability: being out of balance
2: loss of emotional or intellectual poise

On Sunday night at Training Union, Mrs. Shehane is handing out pieces of orange construction paper for us to take home and illustrate this week's Bible verse. She starts to hand me a sheet, but I hold up my index finger with two Band-Aids wrapped around it. "I cut it with a knife," I say, which is a lie. I bit my fingernail to the quick and it hurts like hell.

"Ooh, I hope it gets better." The phony honey drips off her words.

I still can't believe how Mrs. Shehane and all those other stuck-up church members treated the whole family this morning after Preacher Smoot announced my Spelldown victory and invited us to stand in front of the congregation. Usually, people at church pity us. But as the members of the congregation shook our hands and congratulated us, Preacher Smoot beamed as if we had been cured of leprosy.

Mrs. Shehane starts harping about how we are all supposed to practice every single day for next week's big Bible Drill. If I had been in charge of publishing the Bible, I would have arranged the books alphabetically. It's hard as hell to remember where everything is. Every night, Mama calls out five different Bible verses so I can practice finding them. Not because I think God is clocking me with a stopwatch—I just love to win.

Finally, the bell rings, signifying it's time for preaching. I put on my red coat and run down the steps of the education building. It's freezing and smells like it's going to snow, so I pull the hood of my new coat around me and walk toward the front of the church, looking for Daddy. Since the camping debacle, he's been coming with us to morning and evening services on Sundays. But Mama stayed home with the twins tonight. She's not herself lately. Gloria Jean says Mama is going through the change, which is like going through puberty backward.

I find Daddy sucking on a Camel in front of the sanctuary. He looks tuckered out from being good.

"Hey, I'm going to sit in the balcony," I say.

"You know your mama don't allow that," he says, pretending to be stern.

"Please, I promise I'll be real quiet. No one will even know I'm up there."

"Go ahead, skedaddle," he says with a smile, but he's acting fidgety as if a drunk is trying to crawl out of his skin.

The vestibule is empty, so I sneak through the door that leads to the balcony. As I climb the dark, creaky staircase, I count each of the fourteen steps so I won't be afraid. Ever since I was little, I've had nightmares about climbing these stairs. But in the dream I'm naked, and the stairs become narrower and go on forever, until I'm standing on tiptoe on the tiniest step to Nowhere. And when I wake up, I'm always exhausted.

I sit on the front pew in the dark balcony and listen as Mr. Carnes gives the attendance report. One hundred and eighteen people showed up tonight. I hope the sermon is short and punchy. Sometimes on Sunday nights Preacher Smoot leaves out the fifteen minutes of begging at the end of the sermon, neglecting to mention that the unsaved might die on the way home and wake up in *h-e-l-l*. Thank God we aren't scheduled to eat Jesus' flesh or drink his blood—that always takes an eternity or two.

The congregation is singing "Turn Your Eyes Upon Jesus." I know this one by heart. It sounds like a march and funeral song put together. I join in on the third verse. "Turn your eyes upon Jesus, look full in his wonderful face, and the things of earth will grow strangely dim in the light of his glory and grace, in the light of his glory and grace."

Then Preacher Smoot starts telling the story about Paul getting zapped by a magical light on the road to Damascus. I'm not in the mood for one of those zapped-by-God stories. I decide to work on my Latin. I take a church bulletin and a pencil from the pew, and on the back of the budget I write down some of my favorite phrases and their meanings:

> *filius nullius*—a bastard
> *Via Crucis*—the Way of the Cross
> *Via Lactea*—the Milky Way
> *Via Dolorosa*—the Way of Sorrow

> *theatrum mundi*—theater of the world
> *quaere verum*—seek the truth
> *natale solum*—native soil
> *nascentes morimur*—from the moment we are born, we die
> *veni, vidi, vici*—I came, I saw, I conquered

The last one is the motto of Karlene the Conquerer: Veni, vidi, vici.

Finally, Preacher Smoot stops preaching and gives all sinners a chance to get saved. As the congregation sings the first verse of "Just As I Am," I slip down the stairs and walk to our old gray station wagon parked out front on the shoulder of the highway. In the moonlight it looks like a sleeping elephant. I jump into the front seat, hoping I won't have to wait long.

I look out at the strange intersection of Highway 200 and High Street, and feel as if I'm seeing it through fresh eyes. Everything looks so vivid and colorful. So Full of Life. Across from the drive-in theater, the Jiffy Grill is hopping like it's Saturday night. Hoodlum boys sit in shiny cars with their teased-hair girlfriends, eating cheeseburgers and fried onion rings.

On the opposite corner from the Jiffy is Red Clover Toyland, which has a giant toy soldier sign out front. All my life, that toy soldier has stood at attention and saluted me every time I pass. The soldier's uniform used to be bright royal blue and the plume on his helmet was deep purple, but now the colors are faded. The white signpost that holds the soldier up used to be a measuring stick for Red Cloverians to mark the height of their children. Mama measured me several times, but a few years ago, the toy store closed, and people quit measuring their kids.

There's a knock on my window. Billy Ray is standing outside with his Brownie camera around his neck. I roll down the window and the flashbulb explodes. "Hey—you trying to blind me?"

"No, just wanted to get a picture of the Shirley County Spelling Champion," he says, looking handsome in his Red Clover Junior High letter jacket. "Sorry I couldn't make it to the Spelldown. I had to work."

"That's okay. You been to Freewill?"

"Yeah. I had to give the sermon tonight for Youth Sunday. Granddaddy's still trying to talk me into becoming a preacher."

"It sure is weird what some people want," I say.

"Yes, it is, but I don't plan on being a preacher, or staying in Red Clover. I'm going to college or join the navy or Peace Corps or something," Billy Ray says in a dreamy voice.

"Send me a postcard." I roll my eyes.

"You're in a fine mood."

"I'm sorry. It just gripes me how people always talk about leaving Red Clover but never do."

"Well, we'll make it out of here, someway, somehow." Billy Ray smiles.

"You know what? You are absolutely right, Billy Ray Jenkins!"

A sad puppy-dog smile flitters across his face. "Daddy shot up the trailer and took off again."

"Shot up the trailer! What in the world is wrong with—"

"Sheriff will find him. Always does," he says. "But I'd prefer not to discuss it if you don't mind."

"I don't mind at all." I take his hand and squeeze it. He squeezes back.

"I gotta get home, anyway. Tell your mama I said hey." He walks away.

A few minutes later Daddy jumps into the car. "Was that Billy Ray?"

"Yes, sir."

He flashes the headlights and drives the car up the shoulder of the road until he reaches Billy Ray. I roll down my window and Daddy leans over and says, "How about a ride, son?"

"That's okay, Mr. Bridges. I don't mind walking. It's out of your way."

"Get in, son. Ain't nothing in this world out of my way."

Billy Ray shrugs, then hops into the backseat.

"Those onions smell good," Daddy says, like he's all full of energy.

He whips into the Jiffy lot and parks the car in front of Mickey's. The bait shop is closed on Sundays, but an OPEN sign hangs in the window. Above the front door, SCHLITZ glows in neon letters.

"Wait in the car, baby."

"Aw, Daddy, why can't I come in?"

"The Jiffy ain't no place for a girl. Come on, Billy Ray."

Billy Ray and Daddy head toward the Jiffy.

I jump out of the car and yell, "Get Mama a banana milk shake," and then go sit on the hood of the car.

The cold seeps through my coat, my corduroy skirt, my panties, and freezes my butt. I pull up my hood and watch the girls with teased hair smooch their boyfriends. It gives me a horny feeling, so I lie back and look up at the moon hanging golden in the black sky. Staring at the sky reminds me that Earth is hurling and twirling itself through the infinite universe, and that the only thing holding me on to this cold car is a little smidgen of gravity. The vastness of it all makes me realize that being a Baptist is beside the damn point.

"Let's go." Daddy pulls on my scruffed-up black-and-white saddle oxford.

I make Billy Ray sit up front. Daddy pulls out and heads toward town. Not much going on in Red Clover. Just boys riding up and down Main Street, wondering if they will ever find a girl, dreaming about being rich and famous and happy, and hoping most of all that they'll never be like their linthead daddies. Daddy blows the horn at Kelly sitting on the bench in front of the Royal Taxi Cab Company, whittling away. Kelly salutes and smiles.

"Kelly said you might do some driving for him," Daddy says to Billy Ray.

"Yes, sir. After school and in the evenings, during the week." A miraculous image shimmers in my mind of me sitting up front with Billy Ray driving Kelly's taxi.

Daddy turns into the entrance of Whispering Pines Trailer Park, drives down the bumpy dirt road, and stops at a beige trailer with two tall, straggly pine trees in the tiny front yard. The trailer doesn't look too bad. Pieces of cardboard are duct-taped over the living room windows.

"Appreciate the ride, Mr. Bridges." Billy Ray opens the car door.

"Anytime, son." Daddy hands Billy Ray a big white paper bag. "I bought some burgers for you and your mama in case you get hungry later."

"Thanks a lot." Billy Ray takes the bag and walks toward the house.

"See you later, Billy Ray," I call. Then I plop into the front seat.

As I watch Billy Ray kick a pinecone all the way to the trailer, a noisy silence throbs in the car. Daddy looks sorry or guilty about something. His profile looks carved out of stone as he pulls out onto the highway. Then he rolls down the window a little, pushes the lighter in, and fiddles with his cigarettes. The lighter pops out and I grab it like I've done since I was a little girl, then hold it to his cigarette as he inhales the fire into the tobacco. The tires whine on the asphalt as he turns onto Beale Street. He parks in the dirt driveway of a mustardy-colored house. A mangy bulldog charges toward the car, but is yanked back by a chain anchored to a dead oak tree.

"I gotta pick up some cigarettes. Won't take but a minute.

You can listen to the radio." He jumps out of the car and hurries toward the house.

I wish I was anywhere but here sitting in the car, mutilating my fingernails, worrying about why he is going into a trashy house looking for cigarettes instead of stopping at the Esso station we passed a mile back. "Incense and Peppermints" is playing on the radio. I turn up the volume. Strawberry Alarm Clock is by far the weirdest name of a band I have ever heard. I know the words by heart, but listen deeper to see if I can figure out what in the world the song *means*. Maybe it's about dead kings and crippled things. Or about things that smell good. Or about playing games you can't win or lose. Or about turning your eyes inward and taking a real hard look at yourself. Perhaps it's a song about life not meaning a damn thing. That the whole point is that there is no point. It doesn't really matter. The music makes me feel like I'm on a glittery ride to nowhere in particular.

Finally, the car door opens and Daddy slinks into the seat, a brown bag in his hand. The smell of Southern Comfort fills the car. He puts the bag underneath the seat and drives toward home.

We pull into the driveway of our newly painted house that is the color of jonquils during the day, but tonight, in the light of the full moon, it's the color of old teeth. The house is dark, but the porch light is on. Daddy grabs the paper bag from under his seat and walks to the backyard with his head down. The moonlight shines on his face as he lifts the bag to his lips. I hunker down in the car and pray furiously, breaking all of Mama's praying rules. *Dammit God, help my daddy. Turn that liquor into lemonade. Forgive me for being pissed off. Show me the way not to cry myself a damn creek. And oh, yeah, God, thanks for nothing. Nothing at all.*

After I put Mama's milk shake in the freezer, I look out the window and see that Daddy's car is gone. *Damn, damn, damn.* I check on the boys and look in on Mama. She's asleep, one foot hanging off the side of the bed.

I'm nervous as a tick. Standing on my head might calm me down. I grab a pillow from my bed and put it on the floor about ten feet away from my wall of fame. I get into tripod position, then carefully lift my legs into the air. It's weird how I'm upside down, but my heroes still look right side up. Maybe my mind is so used to these headstands that it inverts the image automatically. Ringo's smiling goofily with the big purple heart I colored on his chest. Aretha's dressed in a glittery turquoise dress, her lips almost touching the big, shiny microphone. And in the painting I cut out of my Sunday school book, there's a light breaking through the darkened sky and it's shining on Jesus, who looks willing to hang on that cross forever. The way the artist left off the crown of thorns created a real peaceful effect.

After my brain gets oxygenated, I ease my body down and rest a minute or two. Then I grab our gargantuan flashlight, a towel, and put on my jacket. I walk through the woods to Highway 200. I cross Bear Creek Bridge, then walk past Dodge Country, Buckwheat's Body Shop, and Kentucky Fried Chicken. Across the street, a neon sign flashes RED

CLOVER MOTEL one second and RED LOVER MOTEL the next. That *c* has been acting up for months.

There are no lights on at the parsonage, so I slip around to the back of the church. The window in the kitchen lifts easily and I climb in. I love coming to church when nobody's around. Most times when I sneak in, I just go to the nursery, get a pack of graham crackers, pour myself a cup of orange Hi-C, then go sit in the balcony to admire the stained-glass window of Mary and her baby.

In the sanctuary the sconces along the wall cast a pale yellow light. I adore the clean peachy smell of furniture polish that protects the gray poplar pews. I make my way through the choir room and then to the baptistery, where I strip naked. Then I take three steps down and wade into the small pool. I float on my back in the cool, shadowy water. A huge metal crucifix with grapevines curled around it rises above me. And a buttery light filters down from the ceiling, caressing my skin.

I don't feel angry, or sad, or afraid.

I feel peaceful as a water lily.

After a while I dunk myself real good in the name of the Father, the Son, and the Holy Ghost. Then I just float around in the dark feeling unguilty—like I've never harmed anyone or anything.

13

ne·science

1: lack of knowledge or awareness: IGNORANCE

It's Monday. I'm sitting in the cafeteria, choking down a cold piece of corn bread, feeling like a cadaver in the midst of obnoxiously cheerful students. I couldn't muster up a giggle for a million dollars. I must be sending out a powerful don't-tread-on-me signal. Not one soul has bothered me all morning. I've been trying to finish my history homework, but I'm sad as a bastard, thinking about Daddy's drinking. I wish Billy Ray were here. Last year, whenever I showed up for lunch as The Untalkative One, he'd perk right up and start his happy talk about how one day I'd be President of the whole damn country and he'd be Secretary of the Interior.

To make it worse, Mrs. Harrison is at a conference for Latin teachers. I can't bear the thought of going into her classroom and having to entertain a crummy substitute for fifty minutes, so, after fifth period, I'm going to walk home through the woods.

I look up at the clock. History starts in ten minutes. I read through the short essay Mrs. Helms assigned us to write over Thanksgiving about South Carolina's secession from the Union. Miss Sophia helped me find some original sources, which gave some interesting statistics. The paper sounds convincing, but it's a little too spunky, so I change *dumb-asses* to *morons* and all the *hell*s to *heck*s, then pack my stuff and mosey down the hall with all the other white students to my history class.

When I walk into the classroom and take my seat over by the window, Kim Gainey leans forward and whispers, "Watch out, she's wearing her puke green pantsuit," which means Mrs. Helms had a terribly awful, no-good weekend.

But then I think, *Well, mine wasn't exactly a glorious celebration*. Besides, I'm tired of being the Timid One because I questioned her pronunciation at the bee.

Mrs. Helms sits at her desk with her hands folded and her eyes closed, instead of striding around the room speaking to us in her lecturing voice as she usually does. It's so quiet, you can hear the big square clock ticking. Finally, she opens her eyes. "Instead of proceeding to Chapter Eight, I'd like to ask for volunteers to come up to the front and read their essays to the class." She's speaking in her swing-low-sweet-chariot, coming-for-to-carry-me-home voice.

No one raises a hand. Most students are looking down at their desks or scribbling in their notebooks. Since the mispronouncing incident, I've been waiting until last to volunteer, so as not to appear arrogant. But I really want to read my essay. The second hand on the clock jerks to seventeen minutes past one. Mrs. Helms clears her throat twice and asks for volunteers again. I raise my hand high. She looks around the room, avoiding my row by the window. No one else raises a hand. Mine is still in the air. Desi looks at me and shrugs, as if to say, *She's all yours*.

Kim passes me a note. I unfold it and read: *You're humming real loud!*

Damn it all to hell. I feel embarrassed about my stupid "Kumbaya" quirk, but I force myself to squelch that emotion. The clock's hand jerks to eighteen minutes past one. I stand up beside my desk. "Excuse me, Mrs. Helms, I'd be happy to read my essay." Her eyes look semi-glazed.

"Why, I am not one bit surprised, Karlene," she says in a scary gleeful voice. "You're always *so terribly happy* to read your essays."

Blood swooshes through my heart as I look around the room. The other students don't know what to think. Neither do I, so I pray for courage and walk to the front of the room.

"Mrs. Helms, this was a terrific assignment. I learned a lot from reading about the subject." I breathe deeply, and then with all the gumption I can muster, I read the words scrawled on the raggedy notebook paper:

A Crying Shame

People the world over think of South Carolinians as traitors, morons, and cotton pickers. I cannot bear to think how great South Carolina might have been if those ignoramus politicians hadn't divorced themselves from the rest of the country a hundred years ago.

John C. Calhoun is one of the most infamous South Carolinians. He was the vice president of the United States, but he left that job to become a senator for South Carolina, so he could fight for the right to own slaves. I don't know why he would do such a stupid thing. He had not been pro-slavery before. I figure Mr. Calhoun's buddies must have loved having slaves on their plantations, and they must have persuaded him to use his lawyering skills to keep the slaves enslaved.

In 1860, South Carolina had a white population of 291,000 and a slave population of 412,000! The fact that the government of South Carolina tried like heck to keep almost 60 percent of the population enslaved is pathetic. South Carolinians are stubborn by their very nature and don't admit mistakes willingly or unwillingly. That stubbornness is a trademark of our ignorance.

*It is no great surprise that the
United States government has had a
heck of a time getting this state's
ignoramus politicians to obey the
desegregation laws of the United States
of America. Our local leaders claim
that, by next year, the Shirley County
schools will be desegregated. All I
can say is that I hope to God they
swore on a stack of Bibles.*

The room is quiet as a graveyard after a snowstorm. The students look enthralled. *I hope to God they swore on a stack of Bibles* ricochets inside my head. I turn to hand my paper to Mrs. Helms. Her head is resting on the desk. I can't see her face, but her shoulders are shaking.

I touch her arm gently. "Ma'am, are you all right? Can I get something for you?" She's sobbing softly. I put both arms around her shoulders and whisper, "It's okay, Mrs. Helms, you're just having a bad day. It's going to be all right."

She lifts her head and looks at me with the eyes of a child who's been lost for years. My heart gets a cramp as I see her deep loneliness.

"Come on, Mrs. Helms. You need some rest."

She looks at me with complete trust and stops crying.

"Desi, Mrs. Helms is not feeling well. Will you please help me get her to the lounge?"

Desi walks over and stands on the other side of her. We arrange her arms around our shoulders and help her stand up. Then we escort her out of the room. Ever so softly, I hum "Kumbaya" to comfort her frazzled nerves.

When I reach home, the Plymouth is in the driveway, which means Daddy didn't go to work. My mood swings lower. I shouldn't have gotten my hopes up about Daddy. I throw my books on the floor, flop onto the sofa, and smother my face in the brown vinyl. Poor Mrs. Helms. She wouldn't let me leave her side until her scary husband showed up to take her to the doctor or wherever. I didn't want to let her go with him. Who knows what's in people's hearts. She's not mean or hateful, just horribly sad. She probably keeps her face in a jar by the door like Eleanor Rigby.

I hear the twins' bus stopping in front of the house. I lift my head, wipe my face with my shirtsleeve, and stop crying. Noah and Josh come bouncing into the house. When they see my face, they run over, and Josh asks me what's wrong, with that little worried frown of his. I curl up in a ball and cry some more. They huddle up against me on the sofa and start crying too. They're not used to seeing me so despondent in the afternoon.

A while later the twins are running around in the backyard. When I thought about Mama coming home to a big crybaby and a drunk husband, I washed my puffy face, then fixed the twins a snack and straightened up the house. When I heard

Daddy yell out "Shit!" a couple times, I checked on him and found him agitated and wheezy, but still asleep. I woke him up and made him take a sip of water.

I go into my room and grab the Gund clown Mama gave me for my thirteenth birthday. I named her Elka. She's my crying buddy. She only cost one book of stamps, which has turned out to be a real bargain. Last year, when I opened the present and read the note, *To my little clown*, written in Mama's scribbly handwriting, I realized that I had the key to Mama's laughing place.

As soon as Mama gets home from work, she walks into my room, sees my face, and hears Smokey Robinson crooning "There's some sad things known to man—but ain't too much sadder than—the tears of a clown." She lifts the needle of the record player, turns it off, then walks to the living room. She picks up the phone and dials it. All I can hear her say is ". . . needs some help." A few minutes later, she comes to my door, dressed in her old black slacks and white blouse. "We're having oyster stew for supper," she says in her nip-this-in-the-bud voice, and closes the door.

Mama amazes me. Since I won the Spelldown, she's acting all fired up, like she believes in miracles. And even though she has worked all day and Daddy is drinking again, she's cooking my favorite soup. Lots of times, she makes it after my crying jags.

Someone knocks on my door and I open it. It's Kelly.

"If you have a minute, I'd like to talk with you," he says.

"Yes, sir, I'll be with you in a minute." I walk to the

bathroom and wash my face again. Kelly sure has a way about him. I heard his testimony last year at a special AA meeting when he got his ten-year chip. He talked about how he had been the proudest, hard-drinkingest, God-defying colored man in South Carolina. That was until Old Colonel High gave him a job and introduced him to the Twelve Golden Steps of Alcoholics Anonymous. The sad part of the story is that Colonel High started drinking again and crashed his airplane into one of the Great Smoky Mountains.

In the living room, Kelly is sitting in the Naugahyde recliner talking to Mama, who's sitting on the edge of the sofa. "Excuse me," she says. "I need to check on the stew."

I sit on the couch and Kelly talks to me in his deep, buttery voice, asking about my spelling and what's going on at school. I tell him about Mrs. Helms's breakdown and how disappointed I am in myself that I never got past her haughty ways and saw how tender her heart was. He says I handled the situation the best I knew how. Then I tell him about Daddy. He talks for a while about how living in this world isn't always a pleasure, and that sometimes it's our trials and tribulations that teach us who we really are. Deep down inside, he says, Daddy is a good man, but he's got an affliction he can't solve by himself. He says Daddy was sincere when he asked God to help him stop drinking, but Daddy hasn't learned to let God *stay in the picture*.

It's sort of like spelling, he says. You have to keep working at it. You can't ever give up.

14

ex·ac·er·bate

1: to make worse (pain, disease, anger)
2: to make more violent or severe

On Friday afternoon I hack down a misshapen cedar from the woods with an old butcher knife and drag it toward our house. I have a bad case of *taedium vitae*, which sounds downright cheerful compared to the English translation—weariness of life. The super-duper Kotex slipping and sliding in my panties isn't helping my mood one damn bit. Plus, my hands and arms itch something awful from hauling the tree all the way from Bear Creek. Christmas is only four days away, and the way it looks around here, it's up to me to make the holiday happen. Daddy is God knows where, doing God knows what. Mama's gone to Psalm 91 Beauty Salon to have her hair fixed, and then to buy groceries.

But at least I have Mrs. Harrison. When she brought me home from school today, she offered to watch the twins while I cut down a tree. As I drag the cedar toward the front porch, she's looping red ribbon into a big bow. The twins squeal like piglets when I plop the tree up against the house.

Mrs. Harrison looks up. "You got a nice, big one."

"Big enough, I reckon. Not too ugly, either," I say in my martyred voice.

"It's perfect." She gives me a quit-feeling-sorry-for-yourself look.

If it weren't for Mrs. Harrison, I'd have sunk into this dunghill of a life. When I finally told her about Daddy's drinking, she said she was familiar with that type of situation. She said I was lucky to have something as grand as the spelling bee to focus on. Now, when she drops me off from spelling practice, she often chats with Mama.

"Hey, Jelly Bean, I have to leave." She hands me a package wrapped in silver foil with a red satin ribbon. "An early Christmas present." For a second I feel like boo-hooing, but I choke it back. She rises from the porch step. "Save it for later. It's just a little something." She grabs me and hugs me hard. I squeeze her back, wishing I could go home with her.

"Come on, you little knuckleheads," she says to Josh and Noah. "Escort the queen to her chariot." Laughing, they run in circles around her all the way to her station wagon. "Hey, call me later if you want to talk," she yells, then drives away, tooting the horn.

I put the tree in our old red-and-green Christmas tree stand. It leans a little to the right, but it will have to do. A crooked Christmas tree isn't the worst thing in the world. After I drag the tree into the living room, I make an afternoon snack. The house feels peaceful with just the three of us munching on our peanut butter crackers and sipping hot cocoa at the kitchen table. But I notice the twins need a haircut. Until recently, Mama has always kept them looking like the little boys in the Sears catalogue. I've been trying to keep our family shaped to Mama's standards, but trying to do things the Lila Bridges way wears my nerves to a frazzle.

Mama has always complained about being at the end of her rope, but I can tell she's almost ready to turn the rope loose. She goes through the same motions as before. Work. Church. Sleep. But she's about quit eating anything except cornflakes, and her sick headaches come more often and last longer. My parents have fallen back into their old routine. They work every day on different shifts and they sleep in the same bed, but they hardly speak to each other. Daddy still spends most weekends someplace else, showing up drunk on our doorstep late Sunday night. But at least he makes it to his loom-fixing job almost every day, which keeps us out of the Poor House.

After the twins finish their snack, they beg to decorate the tree. I tell them they have to take their baths first, and put on their pajamas. While they play in the tub, I curl up on the sofa and—

Something strikes my cheek. I must have dozed off.

"Yee-haw!" Noah screams, standing at the door swinging a huge sanitary pad like a slingshot.

I jump up and slip on several pecans on the floor, falling flat on my butt. Noah fires more pecans at me and runs away. I chase him into the kitchen and find Josh wearing a giant purple Kotex box on his head, with holes cut in it for his eyes. He's stomping around with his arms held out stiff like he's Frankenstein. Unable to see out of the eyeholes, he's banging into everything. Sanitary pads are strewn all over the floor. Noah has jumped on top of the table and is slinging pecans from his Kotex slingshot. A pecan whizzes by my ear and strikes the Kotex Frankenstein. I yank the stupid box off Josh's head, jerk the pad from Noah's hand, and scream, "I'll kill you if you touch this stuff again."

"What are those things?" Josh asks.

"It's private lady stuff, that's what it is." I don't know how to tell them about blood and babies and all that icky stuff that happens to girls. Why did the Kotex people make their dumb boxes so gargantuan and in that impossible-not-to-notice purple? This is the final humiliation. Tomorrow, I'm buying the Tampax. I'll master tampon insertion if it kills me.

"Josh." I dangle the sanitary napkin in the air. "Pick up the rest of these and put them back in the box."

"Noah, you pick up all the pecans and put them in the bag. Then get that box of construction paper and crayons and go sit at the kitchen table with your brother. Draw Mama a Christmas tree. I don't want to hear another sound from either of you. You understand me?"

The boys set about doing as they are told.

Before Mama gets home, I want to make sure the tree is decorated and supper is ready. She has always made home-cooked meals, but for the first time in our family's history, our freezer is filled with Dixie Darling–brand TV suppers, chicken potpies, and frozen French fries.

We'll decorate the tree first. I climb the rickety hideaway stairs to the attic and bring down several old hatboxes full of ornaments and a large cardboard box with tangled strands of

Christmas lights. I call for the boys and let them help. Only one string of lights works, and I wrap it around the unfortunate tree. We take turns placing all the homemade and dime-store ornaments on the branches. From a green silk pouch I pull out the ornament Mama calls an heirloom. She got it at the stationery store, back when she had the Christmas spirit a few years ago. It's a miniature red book made out of wood. *A Christmas Carol* is written on the front in gold letters, and on the back cover is the inscription *God bless us all. Each and every one.* I hang it high, out of the twins' reach.

Instead of making the twins place the silver foil icicles individually on the tree, I let them throw them in clumps that now hang crookedly over most of the branches. I pull out the creamy-faced ceramic angel in a starched white dress from a cardboard box. One of the wings is hanging by a thread. I tape it to the angel with masking tape and then stand on a chair and place it at the top of the tree. I jump down, turn off both lamps, and stand with my little brothers, admiring the tree as it twinkles in front of the picture window.

I hear a car pull into the driveway. "Shh. Let's surprise Mama." I peer through the blinds and see Kelly putting the grocery bags on the front porch. When Mama comes into the room, she looks startled. A peace-on-earth look flashes across her face for half a second, then disappears.

The twins help bring in the groceries, and then they play quietly in their room while I make a big pot of oyster stew just like Mama's, with lots of evaporated milk, butter, and pepper. For the boys, I make fried bologna sandwiches. I set the table and find two half-burned red candles and light them.

The three of us children eat quietly, watching the tiny soup crackers grow soggy in Mama's barely touched stew. She thanks me for cooking such a good supper and then takes a long, hot bath and goes to bed. I get the twins situated on a blanket in front of the TV to watch an episode of *Get Smart* with that stupid Maxwell Smart and sexy Agent 99.

After I wash the dishes I decide it is a good time to better familiarize the twins with the real Christmas story, so I climb into the attic and lug down the rectangular pine box with the Holy Family inside. I carefully unwrap each figurine: the three Wise Men, Mary, Joseph, and the animals, and put them on the kitchen table with the manger. Baby Jesus is missing.

The boys run into the kitchen and want to play with the Holy Family. The figurines are made of sturdy plastic, so I say okay, then climb back into the attic to search for Jesus. I fumble through layers of yucky insulation, but can't find him. I sit down on a piece of plywood and rack my brain trying to figure out what might have happened to the figurine of the pretty baby. Downstairs, Josh and Noah are mooing like holy cows, baa-baaing like holy sheep, and cock-a-doodle-dooing like holy roosters. Their frolicking reminds me that some people are born happy.

When I come down, both boys are standing on the kitchen counter. Mary and Joseph are wearing GI Joe parachutes. Noah tosses Mary so high into the air that she hits the ceiling and crashes to the floor. When Josh tosses Joseph into the air, the parachute opens perfectly, allowing Jesus' daddy to float gently to the kitchen floor. I try my hardest not to laugh. They scurry down from the counter, pick up Mary and Joseph, and hand them to me, sly grins on their faces.

The Jesus part of Christmas will have to wait.

I grab one of the red candles and escort the boys to their room. They both climb onto the top bunk and beg me to recite "The Night Before Christmas." I light the candle, then Josh flips off the light switch. I lose myself in the story. Each word glides from my lips and swirls around my little brothers. I don't even stumble on that clunky sentence right before Santa shows up, "The moon on the breast of the new-fallen snow gave a lustre of midday to objects below." By the end of the third recitation, they are asleep. I'm too tired to move one of them, so I leave them together on the top bunk.

I go sit on the sofa in the dark, looking at the tree. Except for the cedar scent, it doesn't smell like Christmas at all. I miss Mama's happy, busy smell mixed in with the smell of cinnamon. For holidays, baking the right cakes and pies has always been as important to Mama as having the right clothes. Every year, like clockwork, she bakes fruitcake for Christmas, almond pound cake for New Year's, red velvet cake for Valentine's Day, fresh coconut cake for Easter, cherry pie for July Fourth, pumpkin pie for Halloween, and sweet-potato pie for Thanksgiving.

This is the first December in my life that Mama has *not* spent every spare moment in the kitchen making fruitcakes for Christmas. I don't exactly like fruitcake, but every year I help her by grating fresh coconut, shelling pecans and black walnuts, and chopping dates and figs into tiny pieces.

In the kitchen, I open the cabinet and pull out the gigantic Sunbeam Mixmaster. Another one of Mama's Green Stamps prizes. It's white with glossy black trim and has twelve speeds. Looks like a little cement mixer for the kitchen. Cost seven books of stamps. I pasted every one of those stamps myself, and feel like the mixer is half mine.

I put on Mama's green bib apron with bright white daisies. As I flip through my grandma's batter-splattered cookbook looking for the sugar cookie recipe, it hits me full force that I never even had a grandmother. Daddy's mama keeled over from a heatstroke while banging the piano in church one Sunday morning. Mama's mama had one of her breasts gobbled up by cancer. Their pictures sit on opposite ends of the mantel in the living room. My daddy's mama looks peaceful, as if she's sure of heaven. Mama's mama looks riled up about something. The cookbook I'm using is the riled-up one's. I'd love to have a grandmother, even if she were cranky. I find the cookie recipe on page 118 and place the rolling pin over the page to hold my place.

Headlights beam in the yard, and a car door slams shut. I hear Daddy's muffled voice at the front door and run to the living room. Kelly is lugging Daddy across the threshold.

"Just lay him on the rug, Kelly," I say. "He can sleep there tonight. I don't want him to wake Mama up."

Kelly lays him onto the green-and-red-striped runner. "I'll move him away from the door a bit." He pulls the rug against the wall. "Got a blanket?"

I pick up a pillow embroidered with poinsettias and toss it to him. "Just put this under his head. I'll get him a blanket later."

Kelly lifts Daddy's head and slides the pillow under it.

"Want something to drink?" I ask.

"No, thanks. Got to be getting back to the station." Kelly stands at the front door like he wants to say or do something.

"Why did it quit working?" I ask.

"Why did what quit working?"

"The Twelve Golden Steps and all that malarkey."

"The program didn't quit working, your daddy quit working the program. He still thinks he can get relief from the bottle. It's normal to relapse. Just keep praying for him."

"Thanks for bringing him home."

"You're welcome," Kelly says, then nods his head toward the picture window. "Mighty pretty tree you got there." He leaves, closing the door behind him.

I tiptoe into the twins' room and find the shabby gold electric blanket in the closet. I plug it into the outlet in the living room, turn it on low, and spread it over him. I sit on the sofa. Daddy's face looks like a little boy's, dreaming of his mama.

Mrs. Harrison's gift glimmers under the tree. I wonder what the Harrisons are doing tonight. Probably driving up to Charlotte for the Singing Christmas Tree or having a candlelit supper at home. I might as well open the present. The bow comes loose with one tug. Inside is a handmade card with a Christmas tree colored by Celia. Inside, the card reads *Adeste Fideles*. I poke through the tissue paper and pull out an ornate silver music box. I open it and chimes start playing "O Come, All Ye Faithful." After it stops, I turn the key and listen again and again.

The music lightens my spirit and thrusts me into the future. I see myself going to Duke University, becoming a doctor, moving to Africa, and doing Jesusy things, like Albert Schweitzer. Or sailing to China, feeding the hungry, and eating with chopsticks, like Pearl S. Buck. Whatever I do, it will probably be on another continent.

I close my eyes and feel like a million sparklers are inside my head. A vision comes to me of twelve angels in blue velvet robes, perched right on top of the house. A few of them have harps. A few have trumpets. One has cymbals, and she's smashing them together. Mary's up there too, floating around with her baby, who has a gold shimmer around his little body.

A knock at the door interrupts my vision. I open the front door. Billy Ray stands there in his Midway Theater outfit, smiling. "Heard about your spectacular tree."

"Come in. You can help me make cookies."

He comes in, then walks over and checks on Daddy.

"Just another Friday night at the Bridges house," I chirp.

"At least he's safe at home." Our eyes meet. I'd like to cut my tongue out. Crawdad's in the county jail for passing bad checks.

In the kitchen I give him a bowl, some flour, and the sifter. "You're in charge of the dry ingredients." Then, as I cream the sugar and butter together, I tell him all about the paratrooping business and how Baby Jesus got lost in the attic.

15

ame·lio·rate

1: to make better or more tolerable

As I pack my pajamas into the new suitcase, I write the obituary in my head:

> While preparing for the South Carolina State Spelling Bee, Karlene Kaye Bridges, an eighth grader from Red Clover Junior High School, accidentally spelled herself to death. Her teacher, Mrs. Amanda Harrison, said her student had been complaining of severe brain cramps for several days before her head exploded.

Imploded is a better word to describe how my head feels. But at least I have my very own Samsonite suitcase. It's cherry red with a gray silk lining. Mama gave it to me for Christmas, traded in five books of Green Stamps for it.

It's a miracle, but we made it through another Christmas. Gloria Jean and Wendell insisted we come to their house on Christmas Day. Mama got pretty emotional when she saw Gloria Jean had cooked the traditional meal: turkey with corn bread dressing, giblet gravy, cranberry sauce, green beans with fatback, sweet-potato casserole with marshmallows on top. She even made one of those icebox fruitcakes with graham crackers and condensed milk that you don't even have to cook. Thank God, Daddy stayed halfway sober.

Finally, it's the middle of January. Tomorrow is the state spelling bee. As soon as I finish packing, Mama, Daddy, and I are driving to Anderson to stay at Howard Johnson's, about a hundred miles from here. I press hard on the top of my suitcase and close the latches. There's a piece of callused skin on my thumb that's aggravating me, so I yank it off with my teeth. Blood oozes from the tiny rip. I suck my thumb. The blood tastes rusty and sweet.

Since I won the Shirley County Spelldown, my nail-biting habit has gotten a lot worse. Now I'm chewing the skin around my nails. I can't help it. Mama used to dip my fingers in garlic salt and castor oil to keep me from biting them. But it never worked. Some people pick their noses. Some smoke cigarettes. Some pray too much. Some drink too much. I chew things that aren't supposed to be chewed. Daddy calls me Chipmunk because I mutilate my pencils.

"Did you pack your pumps?" Mama says, standing at my door, wearing her charcoal gray slacks and white wool sweater. Every hair is in place, lipstick perfectly applied, cheeks lightly rouged. No matter how much Mama gets on my nerves, I always know I'm in the presence of a lady.

"Yes, ma'am, I packed them," I say, sucking on my wounded thumb.

"Good. What about your new tights?"

"I packed them."

"Just wanted to make sure." She walks back to the living room.

Mama's been in a twitchy mood ever since last night, when she caught me reading *Tanya Marie's Enlightened Guide to Astrology and the Tarot*, a thick book I bought at the dime store a while back that also included a deck of tarot cards. She started sermonizing on how it wasn't good for me to read those hocus-pocus books. Not a single one of them even mention the Lord. I ought to get to the bottom of the religion I was born into instead of dillydallying around with that nonsense, and that since I was born in South Carolina, God intended me to be a Christian. Otherwise, I would have been born in China or India or Africa.

"Don't forget, you promised to call Mrs. Harrison," Mama hollers.

I rush to the living room, pick up the phone, and dial the number, sucking my aching thumb. Mama's sitting on the sofa reading the *Baptist Courier*. The phone rings four times before Mrs. Harrison says hello. "Hey, Mrs. Harrison. We're leaving in a few minutes. Just wanted to let you know."

"Bless your little pointed head, I was just thinking about you. Go show them what you're made of, Karlene. Vowels and consonants. Consonants and vowels. Always in the right order."

"You still coming tomorrow?" I ask.

"Is a sheep sheepish?" she says.

"Baa-aah, baa-aah," I bleat. Mama just shakes her head and keeps reading.

Mrs. Harrison laughs. "See you tomorrow, Ace."

When I put down the phone, Mama rises from the sofa, slings her purse over her shoulder, and picks up both volumes of the dictionary. "Your daddy wants to get to Anderson by six. You know how riled up he gets. I'm going on outside to keep him company."

"I'll be out in a minute." I rush into the bathroom, open the cabinet, and grab the metal box of Band-Aids. Daddy honks the horn three times. I spill a bunch of Band-Aids into the toilet. *Damn it all to hell.* I pull one from the box, wrap it around my wounded thumb, then flush the fallen Band-Aids down the toilet.

Outside, Daddy's standing at the rear of the car, smoking a cigarette, his foot on the bumper. He takes my suitcase and puts it into the trunk, then slams the lid. "Let's go, Chipmunk." He winks and holds the car door open for me.

The car smells of Aqua Velva and Listerine. *Velva* sounds like something sexy, lickable. Sounds like the words *velvet* and *vulva* mixed together. *Listerine* sounds like something you'd swish around in your mouth to kill germs. Quite unpoetic to name a nasty-tasting mouthwash after Dr. Joseph Lister, who, after all, discovered *a-n-t-i-s-e-p-s-i-s*. I sit in the backseat of the station wagon, feeling soothed by a rare silence that says everything might work out after all.

I gaze at Daddy as he smokes a Camel with one hand and steers the car down Highway 200 with the other. He looks a lot like Lloyd Bridges on *Sea Hunt*. Mama looks like a virgin queen from King Arthur days. From the back they look wonderful together. I feel all hunky-dory, as if I'm in a Norman Rockwell painting titled *Girl in the Backseat*.

When we get to the highway, Daddy steps on the gas to pass a car, and a pint of Southern Comfort slides from under his seat into my territory. At least the seal on the bottle is unbroken. I imagine a big, fat eraser eliminating the bottle from the painting we're in. Then, with my foot, I push the bottle back underneath the seat where it belongs. I have enough of my own crap to worry about. My vocabulary is filled with words I have seen but never heard, and I am afraid I won't recognize them when they are spoken, that some of the letters will be silent and I won't know it, like *impugn*, with that stupid silent *g* that makes the *u* say its name.

I ask Mama for volume *A-K* of the dictionary. I randomly flip to a page and place my finger on a word. *Henchman*, an obedient, unscrupulous follower. *Obedient* and *unscrupulous* don't seem to belong together. Sometimes dictionary definitions are obscure, like this one, and I have to look up the definition of the definition. But I don't want to bother Mama for volume *L-Z*, so I put the dictionary on the floor and lay my head on the seat. A while later I awake in a pool of drool. Daddy has already checked into the motel, and we are parked in front of the restaurant.

The waitress is a pretty redhead with good manners, and she brings our drinks right away. Mama and Daddy sit across the booth from me, sipping their coffee from thick beige mugs. Daddy's eyes look like those of a starving lion that has stepped into a steel trap. His hands are shaking a little. I understand how hard it is for him to be here like this, trying to act like he doesn't want a drink. Mama looks at me as if she has never seen me before. They both order fried chicken, rice and gravy, and green beans. I decide to try something I've never eaten: Salisbury steak with mashed potatoes and mushroom gravy. I've never eaten a mushroom in my life.

The food arrives and looks appetizing, but the mushrooms have the texture of rubber bands and taste like nothing at all. The Salisbury steak is just plain old hamburger meat molded into an oval patty. The mashed potatoes taste like spitballs.

Later that evening, after we settle into the motel room, I walk across the street to Sears. I'm shocked at how big it is. The Sears in Red Clover is just a catalogue store with a few appliances and lawn mowers, but this is a huge department store. I head straight for the toy department, where I fondle a girl's bicycle, then yank the plastic streamers hanging from the handlebars. I wonder what kind of glue holds them so firmly in place. I remember the Christmas I got that pathetic little oven from Sears instead of the bicycle I'd circled and memorized in the Green Stamps catalogue: *A Murray girl's 26-inch deluxe model, turquoise body with chrome fenders and rims, dual headlights, white sidewalls, and waterproof two-tone saddle*. I refused to take the oven out of the box. Eventually, Mama realized Jesus would come back before I baked a precious little cake in the precious little oven, and she shipped it back to Sears.

The smell of fresh popcorn draws me toward a large booth in the center of the store, surrounded by glass containers full of candy corn, jelly beans, chocolate-covered peanuts, peanut brittle, cashews, and *p-i-s-t-a-c-h-i-o-s*. A young man with a crew cut and a *c-o-n-t-a-g-i-o-u-s*-looking case of acne is scooping white puffy kernels from the popcorn machine into bright yellow bags. He looks like an Eagle Scout. YVES BAUKNIGHT is engraved on his name tag. I love when *y* pretends to be a vowel.

"May I help you?" he says in a froggy voice.

"No, thanks, I'm just looking," I say, then slowly circle the booth again, imagining the taste of everything. "How much are the cashews?"

"Forty cents for a quarter pound," he says, looking at me with the prettiest pair of crossed green eyes I've ever seen. I feel sorry for Yves. Maybe I will become an *o-p-t-h-o-m-o-l-o-g-i-s-t* and cure his *s-t-r-a-b-i-s-m-u-s* one day. No, that isn't right. It's spelled *o-p-h-t-h-a-l-m-o-l-o-g-i-s-t*.

I pay for the cashews and head toward the lingerie department, where I spot a display of red bras—the lacy push-up kind made of nylon, with smooth, round cups. Mama buys me those stiff cotton bras with sharp, pointy cups that look like weapons. I grab my size and look around for a clerk, but can't find one. The sign says WAIT FOR ASSISTANCE, but I go into the dressing room anyway.

When I look at the girl in the full-length mirror, I see she's not so skinny anymore. Big, fat, smoochy lips. Dungarees with legs rolled up. Red Clover Tornadoes sweatshirt. No wonder Mama rolled her eyes. I pull my shirt off and look at myself in the mirror. The pointy white bra is pathetic. I remove it and put on the red one that fastens easily in the front. The girl in the mirror has substantial *c-l-e-a-v-a-g-e*! I unsnap the bra and fling it onto the floor. I dress quickly and make my way to the exit. The cold January night embraces me as I head down Main Street.

The marquee above the Visulite Theater spells out THE GRADUATE in big black letters. Holy moly. I love Simon & Garfunkel. Mrs. Harrison plays the sound track all the time. I stare at the poster. A woman is putting on her stockings while a young man stands in the background watching her with *S-E-X* in his eyes. I didn't get to see it last year when it came out because I had tonsillitis. The next movie starts at eight o'clock. I hurry toward the motel. When I pass Lucky's Diner, there is only one customer, a handsome man wearing a fancy suit, sitting on a bar stool drinking coffee, staring out the window. He looks sad, like he's full of rain, so I wave at him. He waves back. I imagine myself a little bit older, walking into the diner, sitting beside him, and acting so mysterious, the poor man falls hopelessly in love with me right on the spot.

When I get back to the hotel room, the door is unlocked, and I rush in to find my parents curled up beside each other on one of the double beds watching Red Skelton on the black-and-white TV. The room smells of cigarettes and White Shoulders, and for a second, Mama and Daddy seem almost happy to be alive. Now that he's broken that seal on the bottle, he doesn't look so tortured anymore.

I give Mama the rest of the cashews and explain how keyed up I feel, and that going to the movies might take my mind off the spelling bee. Mama stalls and looks at Daddy, who hands me five dollars and tells me to be careful. It has never been so easy to get something I want.

A light rain begins to fall as I gallop toward the theater. My basketball shoes slap the sidewalk, breaking up the foggy silence of the night. Being out of Red Clover makes me feel fearless.

In the ticket booth a gypsy-looking woman is rolling quarters in brown paper sleeves. I buy a ticket and walk inside the lobby, where a giant dusty chandelier hangs from the ceiling. I run my fingers across the faded, gold-velvety wallpaper and, for the first time in my life, bypass the refreshment stand. The greasy cashews are scrambling around in my stomach like ladybugs. As I make my way down the aisle, I pass three other loners before taking an aisle seat seven rows from the front. My stomach starts to settle as I watch the Bugs Bunny cartoon.

When the movie finally starts, the music spirals into the theater, making my corpuscles vibrate. It's as if the characters and I are breathing the same air, hearing the same music. I feel like I'm the film spinning through the projector, exhilarated by the light.

I feel out of place, like Benjamin Braddock—the cute boy who just graduated from college, who doesn't know what to do with his life, and who isn't getting any help from any of the dumb-ass adults. My legs feel sexy in Mrs. Robinson's stockings. I like the taste of her cigarette in my mouth. All of it feels delicious and a little bit wrong, but not wrong enough to stop. Their sexual affair makes me think the world is made of *maybe*s. Maybe sins are nothing more than mistakes. Maybe God views people's lives like thrilling movies made in Technicolor. Maybe when he watches, he does *not* measure everything we do or think of doing on a scale from Innocent to Guilty. Maybe he doesn't point a finger at Mrs. Robinson for screwing Benjamin or at Benjamin for being screwed, or at me for wanting victory tomorrow above all else. Maybe I am just like Mrs. Robinson, whom *Jesus loves more than she could ever know.*

But by the end of the movie, I hate Mrs. Robinson for being such a rotten mother, and I'm rooting for Benjamin to crash Elaine's wedding to save her from getting married to that fancy college boy she does not even love. I don't give a hoot about Elaine marrying Benjamin. I just want them to get away and make up their own minds about their lives. At the end Elaine and Benjamin are sitting beside each other on the backseat of a bus. There's this feeling in the air as the bus pulls away—that they're going Nowhere in Particular. I see the sad truth in Elaine's and Benjamin's eyes that their souls are separate *and always will be*. That's the part that really gets to me.

Listening to the music, I watch all the credits, and am the last person to leave the theater. I feel all grown-up, and sad as a bastard. Lucky's Diner is closed, but the sign on the door still says OPEN. I wonder where the lonely diner has gone. Is he staying in the same motel as us, or does he live with his crazy mother? Maybe he's an undertaker haunted by corpses. Maybe he's an angel with broken wings. When I'm real tired, my mind gets warpy about things, supposing this and that. It's been a hard day's night. I feel like sleeping on the sidewalk, but I trudge toward the motel.

16

1: a meaningful coincidence
*2: the coincidental occurrence of events that seem related,
but are not explained by conventional mechanisms
of causality*

The next morning I awake to the smell of coffee and menthol shaving cream. I lie still as a *v-o-y-e-u-r*, soaking up the images of my parents. Mama is dressed in a blue suit, sitting in a yellow vinyl chair, sipping coffee from a paper cup. She's twirling her string of fake pearls around her finger. Her lips move as she reads from her worn Bible. In the bathroom Daddy is pulling a razor across the face in the mirror. Maybe he's having a conversation with himself about not drinking today because it's my special day, not *his*.

Last night's dream flashes in my mind. I am standing on my head on an empty stage before a huge audience. My skirt is flipped over, exposing my panties. Someone asks me to spell a five-syllable word I've never heard before and I'm unable to spell it. Instead, cashews spew like a geyser from my mouth onto the floor. Spectators jump onto their chairs to get away from the puke.

Daddy wipes the streaks of foam from his face. His reflection yells that the bathroom is all mine.

Twenty minutes later I emerge, properly attired in my good-speller's costume: black skirt, white blouse, and yellow sweater. The black pumps squeak as I walk to the car. When Mama sees how I look, she smiles. Mama's an *e-n-i-g-m-a*, a ninth-grade dropout who looks real educated but can't spell a lick. Sometimes I feel ashamed at how words settle into my brain like orphans who've found a good home, without even trying.

While Daddy checks out of the motel, I sit in the backseat of the car and assure Mama that, no, I do not want even one Krispy Kreme doughnut. My stomach churns from sheer emptiness, as if I have vomited up my soul. In the background, Mama drones on with her do-your-best-Jesus-will-take-care-of-everything lecture. I say "Yes ma'am" at all the right places, but Mama's sermonizing makes me wish I'd been born way back before the Lord was born. Finally, Daddy gets back into the car. I smell alcohol. Please let it be Listerine.

When we turn the corner at the Anderson County Library, I make a quick inventory of the parking lot, and spot only one car that is older than our Plymouth station wagon. I look for Mrs. Harrison's station wagon, but don't see it. Then I look for Mr. Harrison's white Cadillac and see it in the first row. The thought of Mr. Harrison sitting in the audience in his fancy business suit makes me feel like puking even more.

I walk behind my parents toward the library. The smell of Mama's hair spray and Daddy's cigarette drifts back to me, and I will myself not to retch. When we reach the door to the library, Daddy hands me a purple rabbit's foot and says, "Good luck, Chipmunk." I say thank you and walk into the library, imagining a three-legged purple rabbit limping around in the world just so I can taste victory.

The old library smells of fresh paint, and the floors sparkle like green glass. Most of the spellers' chairs are already occupied. Good spellers aren't good-looking, as a rule. Most of the kids look over- or underfed, spoiled or neglected, scared shitless or confident. Extreme cases. Not your average, isn't-life-great kind of kids. Mrs. Harrison stands near a chair in the front row that has KARLENE BRIDGES written in large block letters across it. I walk toward her, feeling as if I'm walking three inches above the floor. She hangs a paper sign around my neck with a big number 8 written on it.

"Karlene, honey, just relax and breathe. Say each word to yourself. See the letters appear in your mind one at a time. Then spell it like you see it."

"I thought I'd just try my best not to vomit," I say with my straightest face.

"Good strategy, Ace." Mrs. Harrison walks away and greets my parents standing at the back of the room. She leads them over to some seats in the second row beside Mr. Harrison.

I shake hands with the boy on my left. His name is Timothy Brinkley, and he smells like the King of Mothballs. He's wearing a navy blue wool vest with one of those fakey gold coat-of-arms emblems. Poor kid looks like one of those befuddled geniuses who can't even tie their shoes. He's probably the best speller in the universe. I squeeze my rabbit's foot. Then I close my eyes and see myself waving a giant trophy over my head. The applause almost bursts my eardrums.

Abby Boyce sits to my right. We introduce ourselves. She's from Charleston and has pale skin and black freckles, and she smells like baby powder. Her fingernails are painted a pale pink. I'd give up my eyelashes to have hands as pretty as hers.

The Assistant Superintendent of Something or Other is a tall, skinny pine tree of a man. He thanks an excruciatingly long list of people, from Governor McNair all the way down to Mr. Whitehall, the janitor, but he neglects to mention the parents who birthed the little spelling freaks, or their coaches. The whole room hums in a whizzy kind of silence. I can't feel my butt sitting in the chair. It's like my nerve cells are scattered all over the room.

The first speller, a short, curly-haired girl from Kershaw, spells *xylophone*. The second speller, an athletic-looking boy, misspells *reconnaissance*. The third speller misspells *conflagration*. Spellers 4, 5, and 6 avoid the dreaded bell by spelling *egalitarian, resplendent*, and *bravado*. It's Abby's turn. She stands up, her fingers crossed on both hands.

"Will you please spell *repartee*?" the Giver of Words says.

Abby asks for a definition and learns that *repartee* means making witty remarks or jousting with words. She spells it *r-e-p-a-r-t-a-y*, and the bell rings.

As she walks to take her seat in the audience, I whisper

the new Spelling Prayer I came up with last night: "Dear God, Author of All Emotions, give me VICTORY or give me death." It might be a little sneaky to give the Almighty an ultimatum like that, but I figure he wants me to live a long and prosperous life.

I stand up and the Giver of Words gives me a word. I spell it *d-i-s-a-m-b-i-g-u-a-t-i-o-n* and sit back down. Mrs. Harrison halfway lifts herself out of her chair and salutes me. It will be a long time before I have to spell again, and I'm afraid that watching the sorrow and anxieties of the other spellers will wipe me out, so I let my nerves float around. A phrase from the "The Sound of Silence" plays over and over in my head: the one about people *bowing and praying to the neon God they'd made.*

I look over at my two sets of parents, who are so well dressed. The Harrisons look totally enraptured, but Mama and Daddy look terrified, as if they were watching Daniel in the lions' den. And for the first time, I realize how nerve-wracking it must be for them to have a daughter like me.

Eons pass as spellers spit out letters correctly or incorrectly. Daddy has made three trips outside. Praise Jesus he didn't call much attention when he tripped over the threshold. Spelling is a nerve-wracking business for everyone. With my particles being so wavy and scattered all over the place, I can't concentrate on any spelling words except my own. So far I have managed to spell *ostracization, wanderlust, inimitability,* and *ebullience.* And every time I hear that horrible bell ring, and watch another speller take a seat in the audience, I say to myself, *Dear God, Author of All Emotions, give me VICTORY or give me death.*

After two hours it's down to me and the King of Mothballs. We're standing side by side. I'm breathing in and out, sending energy to my brain cells, which have all gravitated back into my skull. Timothy's breath is very ragged. The Giver of Words removes his suit jacket and mops his brow with a handkerchief like he's been preaching for a couple of days. "Mr. Brinkley, will you please spell _____?" The Giver of Words pronounces a word that sounds like *oshuary*. It has a familiar ring to it.

"May I hear the definition, please?" Timothy's voice squeaks, scratches a hole in the tension. I smell his sweaty fear. I know he's stalling. I admire him for it.

The Giver of Words pronounces the word again. "*Osh-u-ary*: a vault for the bones of the dead."

Centuries pass while the unlucky boy squirms, as if nails were being hammered through his thighs. Finally, he says, "*O-s-h-u-a-i-r-y*."

The bell rings. "I'm sorry, Mr. Brinkley, that's incorrect."

The King of Mothballs' head drops into his hands. His mama yelps in the first row. I stare at the purple stains on my fingers from the rabbit's foot.

"Miss Bridges, will you please spell the word *osh-u-ary*?" the Giver of Words says with a lilting tone in his voice, as if he's Bert Parks asking questions in the final round of the Miss America pageant.

Blood rushes through my tired arteries. If I cut my wrists, words would leak all over the floor. I force myself to breathe deeply, and then seek my teacher's eyes. Mrs. Harrison's wink is full of encouragement.

Hmm. A vault for the bones of the dead—it's from the Latin word *ossuarius—of bones*! My lips part and the letters *o-s-s-u-a-r-y* flow from my mouth.

The Giver of Words pauses briefly. "That's correct, Miss Bridges."

I feel electrified.

The Giver of Words smiles at me. "Miss Bridges, in order to win, you need to spell another word. Will you please spell *Chihuahua?*"

I close my eyes and see Itty-Bitty, Gloria Jean and Wendell's two-pound, seventeen-year-old, ratty little dog, yipping and yapping around my legs. Wendell had gotten her as a puppy, and he loved her to pieces. Gloria Jean was devoted to her too. If Itty-Bitty hadn't died last week, I wouldn't have had to look up *Chihuahua* when I made them a sympathy card. It's one of the craziest spellings I've ever seen. Holy moly. It dawns on me: *If Gloria Jean hadn't married Wendell, I wouldn't have had to look up this ridiculous word!* I open my eyes and say "*C-h-i-h-u-a-h-u-a.*"

"Congratulations, Miss Bridges, you are the new Spelling Champion of South Carolina!" The superintendent shakes my hand.

The audience claps and cheers like they're in a football stadium. With his hands held high above his head, Mr.

Harrison claps wildly and Mrs. Harrison is hollering one bravo after another, but Mama and Daddy are standing totally still and perfectly straight, their faces fierce with pride. Winning tears race down my cheeks. I stick out my tongue and lick them.

17

sty·gian

1: of or relating to the river Styx or the lower world
2: extremely dark, gloomy, or forbidding
3: infernal, hellish

I'm standing by the picture window, watching the twins get on the school bus, wondering whether I should go to school today. For the last couple days, Daddy's been in bed with some kind of flu or something, but Mama can't get him to go to the doctor's. Since we got home from the state spelling bee a few weeks ago, it's been terrible. He hardly eats a thing—he's living off of coffee, cigarettes, and alcohol.

"Karlene!" Mama calls out. I rush into their bedroom and find her sitting on the side of the bed, dipping a washcloth into a bowl of ice water. Daddy's wearing his old blue pajamas and the sheet is halfway twirled around him. His breathing sounds wheezier than last night. I sit on one side of the bed and touch his pant leg. It's soaked with sweat. "Goddamn you!" Daddy says, his eyelids closed but fluttering.

"His fever's gone up," Mama says. "We need to take him to the hospital. Call Kelly and tell him to come quick."

I rush to the phone and call Kelly. Mama asks me to pack a few things, so I round up Daddy's clean underwear, socks, deodorant, toothpaste, and toothbrush, and put them in an overnight bag. By the time Kelly comes, Mama has managed to get a clean pair of work pants and a flannel shirt on Daddy. It takes all three of us to get him to sit up on the side of the bed. Kelly's on one side of Daddy, and Mama's on the other. Daddy's wheezing and coughing. I put his shoes on him, tie the laces, and then help wrap his arms around their shoulders. They drag him out to the taxi, and I jump into the backseat and help pull him into the car. Mama gets in and puts a pillow in her lap, and I lift Daddy's head so it can rest on the pillow.

"Please wait." I run to the house, grab my book satchel, and then jump into the front seat beside Kelly.

"You need to go to school. I can handle this," Mama says.

I turn around and look into her tired brown eyes. "I'm going with you, Mama, and that's that."

An hour later we're still in the emergency room at High Memorial. The nurses don't seem too concerned about Daddy. The gray-haired bossy nurse recognized me from my picture in *The Chronicle*. She congratulated me on winning the state spelling bee. But she's been staring at Mama, probably wondering how such a decent, pretty lady ended up with such a sick, smelly man.

The nurse says there's a terrible flu going around and that Daddy's dehydrated. The IV is restoring his fluids and Dr. Harris is on his way. She seems more concerned with the way Daddy smells than with keeping him alive. But he does smell awfully polluted. It's a burned-up kind of smell, as if a million cigarettes had been dumped in a pond of whiskey and set on fire. Maybe it's the fever that's cooking his insides.

Mama acts decent and respectful to the nincompoop nurse, but I can tell she is ashamed Daddy keeps cussing every few minutes.

Around six o'clock in the evening, I'm pacing at the foot of the bed in Daddy's hospital room, and Mama's sitting in a chair beside him. Dr. Harris left a while ago. He said Daddy's got double pneumonia and they're giving him strong antibiotics to clear it up. They're also trying to keep his fever down.

Daddy sits up in bed and shakes his finger at Mama. "Somebody better get rid of these goddamn soldiers before I have to kill them myself."

"It's okay, Miller, it's okay." Mama tries to soothes him.

He jumps out of bed, rips the IV out of his arm, and starts fighting with one of the invisible soldiers.

"Honey, please." Mama tries to grab him by the arm, but he crouches down and swings his arms wildly as if he's being attacked by vultures. Then he falls on the bed and starts having muscle spasms all over his body. Mama pushes the emergency button.

"I'm going to get somebody now." I race down the hall to the nurses' station and tell the nurse Daddy's having a seizure. One of the nurses picks up the phone and the other one follows me back to the room. Daddy's lying on his side, sobbing, saying that somebody is trying to kill me and the twins. The nurse shoos Mama away, bends down, and talks in a soft but authoritative voice. "Mr. Bridges. We're taking care of everything. Nobody's getting hurt around here."

Daddy closes his eyes, but he's still jerking real bad. The other nurse comes in with a hypodermic and asks us to step into the hall. Mama looks frightened as we wait outside the door.

"Maybe he's allergic to the medicine or something," I say. "I don't know, Karlene. I just don't know." Now Mama is shaking.

The nurse comes out of the room and says she gave Daddy a mild sedative and inserted his IV again, and that he's sleeping. They've called the psychiatrist, who should be there shortly. Mama can wait in Daddy's room until the doctor comes, but I have to go downstairs and wait in the lobby. Halfway relieved, I get my stuff and leave.

People are lined up at the reception desk. A violin solo plays in the background. It's kind of sad and comforting at the same time. I find a quiet couch over near the window. The snow's still coming down. I don't ever remember this much snow. I close my eyes.

I wake up to the sound of people shrieking. Across the lobby, the elevator opens, and the people waiting to get on scatter everywhere. A skinny man, naked as Adam, streaks through the lobby, waving a pair of scissors. People jump out of his way as he runs toward the entrance. The receptionist leaps up from her desk and tries to stop him, but he just zips around her. As he gets closer, I see it's Daddy! He looks terrified, as if he's just escaped the fangs of hell.

I jump up and run toward him, but he sprints to the

massive front door and pushes it open as if it's a screen door. A security guard dashes into the lobby and the receptionist yells, "He just ran out the entrance!"

I'm right behind the guard as he rushes out the front door. He goes right, but I go left—in the direction toward home. It's a moonless night, but the hospital grounds are well lighted. Penny-size snowflakes flutter to the ground. I try to run in the snow, but it's too deep, so I clomp through it looking for a sign of Daddy. In the distance, I hear a police siren. I have to find Daddy before they get here. He can't make it too far like he is. Naked. Barefoot. Running in the deep snow. But I don't see any tracks. He's so skinny now, he might be walking on top of the snow. Up ahead there's a row of hemlocks, surrounded by shrubs, all covered in snow. Underneath the giant tree limbs looks like a good place to hide.

"Daddy!" I yell again and again.

The siren shrieks as the police car slides into the parking lot. Its red flashing light makes the snowflakes look pink. Two officers get out and start tromping through the snow in my direction. I make my way toward the last of the hemlocks. "Daddy! Where are you?"

Twenty feet away I see his naked butt. He's standing in front of a young holly tree, just clipping away like he's a barber trimming someone's hair. I don't want to scare him, so I creep toward him. Red berries are scattered all over the snow. "Daddy, hey, it's me." He turns around, looking startled, but then he recognizes me. "Hey, Lila, I just came by to help out in the weave room." He turns away and starts clipping at the air. He thinks *I'm* Mama and *he's at work*. He thinks he's at work!

"Daddy, it's me, Karlene!" I rush toward him.

But two orderlies run by me, carrying a gurney. "We've got him, miss!" One man grabs Daddy and takes the scissors away, and the other thrusts a hypodermic into his skinny hip. Daddy sort of crumples up and they wrap a big white blanket around him and lay him on the gurney. The siren has stopped, but the red light flashes around and around, bouncing off all the smooth, white snow. Then they buckle him down and carry him away.

Billy Ray walks up and puts his arm around me, and we make our way back to the hospital. "Your mama's inside, talking to the doctor. It's going to be all right." My basketball shoes are soaked. I can't even feel my feet. I'm slinging snot all over the place. Everybody's standing around outside the hospital, acting like they're at a goddamn circus. "It's going to be all right," Billy Ray keeps saying, like a record that's stuck.

"What are you talking about? It's never going to be all right. Never. *Never*. My daddy has lost his mind!" I break away from him and rush into the hospital. Mama is standing on the other side of the lobby talking to the doctor, so I rush over and stand beside them. She doesn't seem to notice.

"Mrs. Bridges, has your husband ever had an episode like that before?"

"*Nothing* like this has ever happened," Mama says in a hushed voice, then hangs her head and cries. I put my arm around her waist and hold her steady. Preacher Smoot rushes over and says he heard about the ruckus while making his nightly rounds. Then he offers his hand to the doctor and says, "Hello, I'm Dr. Smoot Faulkenberry, their pastor."

The doctor shakes his hand and continues. "Ma'am, has Mr. Bridges ever been in a mental institution before?"

Mama's still crying too hard, so I answer for her. "No, sir, but he drinks an awful lot, which causes his behavior to be erratic."

Preacher Smoot steps in. "Mr. Bridges has struggled with his drinking for a long time."

"How long has he been drinking like that?" The doctor looks directly at me.

"My whole life," I say. "At least fourteen years."

Mama turns and looks at me with the sorrowful expression of a mother who forgot that her daughter's birthday was today. I smile my kindest smile, letting her know we had far bigger fish to fry.

"My husband has been drinking steady for at least twenty-two years."

The doctor writes something on his chart. "Mrs. Bridges, I think your husband is going through alcohol withdrawal. It's called *delirium tremens*, and it's causing the hallucinations and convulsions. The strong antibiotics and his body trying to fight the pneumonia probably intensified the withdrawal. We restrained and sedated your husband and have taken him to a restricted room on the eighth floor to get him stabilized."

"What about visitors?" Mama asks.

"No visitors until he gets better," the doctor says.

"What about treatment for the drinking?" Mama says.

"Did your husband serve in the military?"

"Yes, sir. He was in the navy, and served in Korea."

"As soon as the pneumonia clears up, we'll help you make arrangements to get him to the Veterans Hospital in Columbia. They have a treatment program."

"Thank you, Doctor. We appreciate your help so very much," Mama says.

"You're welcome, ma'am. We have your phone number. You should go home tonight." He pats her on the shoulder and looks at me with a kind face. "Both of you need some rest. I'll see you tomorrow." He walks away.

"He's right, Lila. I'm taking you home," Preacher Smoot says, then helps Mama into her ancient black coat. I grab my books, put on my red coat, and follow them through the heavy doors.

Billy Ray's waiting by the taxi. "Mrs. Bridges, Kelly wanted me to pick you up and bring you by the station for a minute before I take you home. He has a few things for you."

Mama gets in the backseat. I sit up front beside Billy Ray, mesmerized by the wipers swishing away the snowflakes. I have a vision of everything that's happened today, but it's all happening right *now*, like a sonic boom of images flashing before my eyes in black and white. I'm helping Daddy into the taxi, sitting in his hospital room, chasing him in the snow, and riding in this taxi all at once. A blackbird is singing in the dead of night. And I'm swirling around in a fiery spiral of perfect joy and perfect sadness. The feeling is hard to bear. It's like being baptized, or being born, or dying, or seeing the ocean for the first time. Having this eternal feeling makes me understand why people like to believe that things happen one at a time, in a fixed place, neatly following the thing before—like pearls strung into a necklace.

The snow has stopped. The wipers stop swishing.

"Here," Billy Ray says, handing me a tissue. I wipe away the tears. As we drive along Main, the street is deserted. This snow is perfect. Not a speck of sleet has fallen.

Billy Ray parks at the curb in front of Royal Taxi and we get out and walk around to Kelly's apartment at the back. "It's awfully late," Mama says. "Are you sure he's still awake?"

"I'm sure." Billy Ray puts a key into the lock and opens the door.

The room is terribly dark. Inside, Kelly calls out, "The power went out, but I found some candles. Come on in."

Mama and I follow Billy Ray into the room.

Kelly is walking toward us. He's holding a big white cake with blazing candles. Mrs. Harrison is right beside him.

They're singing "Happy Birthday" to *Me*.

Billy Ray starts singing.

Then Mama.

If I can bear this moment, I can bear anything.

18

ab·ste·mious·ness

1: voluntary restraint from the indulgence
of an appetite or craving
2: habitual abstaining from intoxicating substances

"Okay, you two, you better behave, or I'll hang you by your big toes when you get home." Mrs. Harrison kisses James, then Celia, and helps them into the backseat of the Cadillac. They're half-asleep, but they giggle when she tickles them under their chins. She closes their door and leans into the front seat and kisses me on the forehead. "And you, my dear, look totally stylish." She's just flattering me; there's nothing sophisticated about my outfit: a maroon poor-boy sweater with maroon checked skirt, and navy blue loafers.

"What about me?" Mr. Harrison revs up the engine.

She sashays around the car in her purple velour robe and kisses him on the lips, then whispers something in his ear.

"Probably be midnight before we get home," he says.

"My heart is already pining for you," she says. But I can tell she's thrilled that we're going to the Clemson-Duke basketball game without her.

Mr. Harrison toots the horn as he drives down the circular driveway, and then turns onto Plantation Drive. It's six thirty in the morning. There's a hoarfrost. Everything looks as if it were covered by a sheer bridal veil. Mr. Harrison fools around with the heater. The shape of his fingernails reminds me of Daddy's. He has a juicy aroma, like a Thanksgiving feast without the turkey.

I sniff my underarm. Smells like wet ashes. I've only worn the outfit once, but since I started menstruating, my body odor is unpredictable. Sometimes, though, my sweat smells good like burnt cinnamon toast.

"You can listen to whatever you like," Mr. Harrison says. The radio's set on a classical station in Charlotte. The Harrisons listen to so much classical music that they call the composers by their first names: Wolfgang Amadeus, Johann Sebastian, Ludwig van.

"Oh, but I love classical music," I lie. I don't exactly love it. I live for soul music. Marvin Gaye, Aretha, the Temptations, the Supremes, Little Richard. All my babysitting money goes straight to Motown.

"Rescue Me" is the first record I ever bought, and lately I've been listening to it over and over. It's by Miss Fontella Bass. Fontella is the prettiest name I've ever heard in my entire life, and her voice sounds full of good loving she's been saving up for a long time. I block out Beethoven's Ninth and sing the song in my head—begging like crazy to be rescued by his tender charms because I'm lonely and blue and aching to pieces with desire.

Mr. Harrison talks about the cold front, then about the Clemson Tigers. Then he starts asking me questions about the National Spelling Bee and which college I want to go to and all that jazz. I figure he'll eventually get around to asking me about Daddy.

Just in case he does, I have my speech rehearsed: *Oh, he's doing well, thank you, sir. He finished up the program at the VA hospital and they found a place for him at Winding Springs, which is an excellent treatment facility for advanced drinkers. They say he might have to stay there for a whole year.*

But he doesn't bring up the subject. Mrs. Harrison probably gave him strict orders to make this a happy, happy day, like the surprise birthday party they threw for me at their house a few weeks ago. Mama and Billy Ray were in cahoots with them. Gloria Jean and Wendell and the twins came. So did Kelly, Desi, Andrea, Kim, and a few other friends. The biggest surprise was Mr. Harrison playing the drums, wearing that floppy wig, pretending to be Ringo.

We've been on the road for quite a while. The kids sleep soundly in the backseat, Celia wrapped in a pink quilt and James huddled in his camouflage sleeping bag. Mr. Harrison's gray wool pants are perfectly creased, but they look real soft. A black cardigan covers his royal blue turtleneck shirt. I try to imagine Daddy in those clothes, driving this fine car, with a nice, thick leather wallet in his back pocket. But all I can see is that skinny naked man clipping at the holly bushes in the snow. It's hard to imagine my daddy ever being healthy again.

Mr. Harrison is the only man I've ever known who smells good at the end of the day, the only man I've ever seen in a tuxedo, the only man who gives me goose bumps and the willies at the same time. I feel like a queen bee without a hive when I'm around him, but he has always acted like a gentleman toward me. I've never heard him curse or seen him get mad or treat his family mean. He is an important man, and I am damn lucky he asked me to go to Clemson with them. But here I am, stinking up the car with my body odor. I wonder if he smells me.

In my head Fontella's song grows louder and louder. She wants him to take her heart and conquer every part of it. Poor Fontella singing her heart out like that tears me up, because there is no rescue.

The front seat of the Cadillac is big as a bed. I love the soft bone-colored cloth upholstery. "How about some music from this century?" Mr. Harrison says, then changes the station to Big Ways Radio in Charlotte. Aretha is spelling out *r-e-s-p-e-c-t*, and telling her man she's got to have some of it, especially at night, before he socks it to her. And she tells him flat out that if she doesn't get just a little bit of *r-e-s-p-e-c-t*, she's gonna be gone—and he's gonna be awful lonesome—without somebody like her to sock it to. Aretha knows she's the prize. I guess that's why she's so confident.

"Have you ever seen the Giant Peach?" Mr. Harrison asks.

"The Giant Peach? What is that?"

"You'll see it for yourself in a few minutes. We're almost there."

Soon I see a water tower that looks like a giant peach. It has WELCOME TO PEACHLAND written across it.

"Holy moly, the peach looks like it has fuzz on it. It's amazing."

"Every time I see it, it shocks me." Mr. Harrison reaches underneath his seat and brings out a box wrapped in gold paper with purple irises on it. "This is for you."

"What for? We already celebrated my birthday."

"It's to let you know how much I admire you."

I take the package and put it in my lap. What have I done for him to admire me? Babysat his kids? Won the South Carolina spelling bee?

"Admire me? For what?"

"For being yourself. For being such a champion in life."

I stare at the present. A sprig of rosemary is laced through the purple bow. I bite my lip to keep from crying. Mrs. Harrison has a big rosemary plant in her kitchen. She uses it in her cooking, but, mostly, she just likes the way it smells. I remove the ribbon. The paper falls away, exposing a brown leather book with gold lettering: *Leaves of Grass by Walt Whitman.* I read the inscription: *To Karlene Bridges, Always remember to celebrate yourself. Good luck. Your friend and admirer, Mr. Harrison.*

My fingers rub the letters he has written. The goodness of the words sends shivers of joy in every direction. I turn the page and recite the first three lines of Mr. Whitman's book out loud like Mrs. Harrison taught me: "I celebrate myself, and what I assume you shall assume, for every atom belonging to me as good belongs to you." Mr. Whitman speaking to me like that tears me up, especially since he is dead.

Mrs. Harrison is the one who bought the present, asked him to inscribe it, and wrapped it. She wants her fine husband to be some kind of father figure to me. Her being so kind makes me feel sort of crummy for having all those horny feelings about Mr. Harrison, but I remember that Latin phrase, *Cogitationis poenam nemo patitur*—Nobody should be punished for his thoughts—and I don't feel so bad.

I look over at my handsome pretend daddy and say, "Thank you."

Mr. Harrison's eyes say *You're welcome*, but I'm sorry at the same time. Sorry he will never be able to kiss me the way I long to be kissed. A part of me still wishes he'd kiss me right now. The devil always shows up when he smells weakness, just like Mama says. I close the book and practice conscious breathing, trying to squelch the terrible longing inside of me. Maybe one of these centuries, Billy Ray Jenkins might recognize I'm a girl whose lips were made to be kissed.

When my insides simmer down a little, I change the radio back to the classical station. Beethoven's violin concerto is playing. According to the road sign, Clemson is fifteen miles away.

I sit close to the door, looking out the window at billboards, factories, and ordinary houses. The air in the car is dry and warm. The music of the violin seeps into my skin and makes me think about the long, hard road of my daddy's life. Why I was born into my particular family is a mystery, and why I got halfway adopted by the Harrisons is another one. But I know that no matter how much I love the Harrisons or how much they love me, I do not belong to them. There is something beautifully wrong about it, something almost tragic. But I won't think about that now—because soon, I'll be sitting with my pretend family in a brand-new coliseum, rooting for the Tigers to win.

19

li·bi·do

1: sexual drive, sexual energy: DESIRE
2: vital impulse; the energy associated with instincts
3: emotional energy derived from primitive biological urges

I drop the needle on my favorite Zombies record, "Time of the Season," and stretch out on my bed to enjoy the deep throbbing feeling the song gives me. The drummer sounds like he's having sex with himself and playing all his percussion instruments at the same time. In between drumbeats there are moans of unbearable pleasure. And then the lead singer, in a deep, throaty voice, asks a girl to give it to him easy, and that if she does, his pleasured hands will take her into promised lands. Then there's a jazzy instrumental part that lasts awhile before the drums and the moaning start again. And then the singer asks the girl who her daddy is and if he's rich or not, and whether he's taken the time to show her what she needs to live. That voice makes me want to be that girl he's talking to right *now*.

But of course I'm not that girl. I am Karlene Kaye Bridges, the *virgo intacto*, lying on my bed in my boring flannel pajamas. I pull out a half-sucked cherry Tootsie Roll Pop from my pocket, unwrap it, and stick it in my mouth. The harder I suck, the better it tastes. There's seven inches of March snow outside. No school today. Even the mill is closed. I've been goofing off, talking on the phone, painting my toenails, looking at myself in the mirror, listening to records, wondering if Billy Ray's going to make it here through the snow.

Mama knocks on the door, then turns the knob. It's locked.

"Karlene, hurry up, it's time to turn the upside-down cake."

"I'll be out in a minute!" I love to watch Mama make the pineapple upside-down cake: melting butter in an iron skillet, placing a layer of pineapples and cherries on the bottom, sprinkling them with brown sugar, pouring the cake batter over the fruit, and putting it in the oven to bake. But I have never been allowed to turn the cake right side up because Mama says the iron skillet is too heavy.

So, I rush to the kitchen. Mama's standing by the big black skillet. "Here, just flip the pan over onto the plate."

My wrists wobble when I lift the pan. Mama reaches around me and places her hands on top of mine, steadying them. Together, we turn the pan gently onto the old turquoise plate. Mama removes her hands. "Now, let it rest a second."

A few moments pass and then I hear a gentle plopping sound.

"Can I lift it now?"

She nods and I lift the pan from the cake and set it aside. The cake is perfectly bronzed and smells like fresh-baked heaven, and the pineapples look like delicious little suns.

"Now you know how to make your grandma's Sun Cake," Mama says in a young voice. The sweet, moist smell makes me want to dig into the cake with my hands and eat the whole thing. Lately I feel hungry all the time, and often find myself in a daze standing in front of the refrigerator trying to find something to satisfy this new, unparticular hunger. Sometimes I eat a half dozen dill pickles and almost a jar of olives before I realize what I really want is a pimento-cheese sandwich.

Someone knocks on the door and I answer it. Billy Ray's standing there with snow all over his black toboggan. "Come on, let's go play."

"I need to get dressed. You want to come in?"

"No, thanks, I'll wait outside," he says.

I rush to the bathroom to wash my face and brush my teeth. My hair looks dull, so I brush it and put it into a ponytail. I pull on my hip-hugger jeans, white turtleneck, and pale yellow sweatshirt, then scrounge around under the bed until I find my raggedy Converse All Stars high-tops. I slip on two pairs of socks before putting on the shoes. I can't find my winter gloves, so I grab the pair I wore last Easter. In the mirror, I see a halfway cute tomboy. I put on my red coat, pull the hood over my head, and rush outside.

Billy Ray's not on the porch, so I run into the front yard looking for him. Suddenly, I am clobbered by one hit after another. Billy Ray's standing beside a mound of snowballs wearing his tight, faded Wranglers. He's laughing at me. I throw my hands down into the snow and turn cartwheels until my feet land, smashing half of the snowballs. I hurl one at Billy Ray's chest, then he runs away. I pick up a few snowballs and take off after him. He runs zigzaggedly up the street trying to avoid being hit, laughing like a madman. Seeing Billy Ray so happy running in the snow conjures up a vision of my poor daddy, standing in the snow, snipping berries off the holly tree. It seems like something that happened two hundred years ago.

At the Randalls' house, several of Billy Ray's high school friends are playing football in the front yard. Lucinda is twirling her baton and throwing it up real high. She sees us and comes over to say hello.

Spencer, her brother, jogs over and asks Billy Ray to play.

"Hey, what about me?" I say.

Spencer tosses the football from one hand to the other like he's hot shit. "You forgot your pompoms!"

"Don't be such a jerk." Lucinda pushes him. "Let her play. She's good."

And the game is on.

I play on Spencer's side. Billy Ray is the quarterback for the other team. Lucinda referees and blows the whistle anytime she feels like it, acting like the Queen of Sheba. If flirting were a sport, she would win the Olympics.

Flirting runs in the Randall family.

Spencer acts all nice to me, asking me questions, like who taught me to play football and what college I plan to attend. I kind of enjoy the attention, but want him to shut up and play football. Billy Ray plays with great intensity, as if he's perturbed because Spencer is flirting with me.

Within an hour Billy Ray has sacked Spencer at least six times and has quarterbacked his team to a 12–0 lead. The snow is really coming down, but I am determined to score. We play for a while, but I cannot get open to save myself.

Finally, I see my opening, and I sprint as fast as I can toward our goal. Spencer sees me and throws a high, arcing pass. I jump into the air and catch it, then make a dash toward the garden hose that marks the goal line. As soon as I cross it, someone grabs me around my calves and pulls me down. Snow fills my nostrils. I look back and see it's Billy Ray who tackled me, so I flip myself over and rub snow into his face. Then, suddenly, he's sitting on top of me, staring at me, his eyes blazing like sparklers. I stare back at him, entranced. Our eyes meet. The snow flits and flutters all around us as if we were captured in a glittery snow globe all by ourselves. My body feels electrified, like it could light up the whole world. Billy Ray whispers, "You look amazing."

Amazing. He said I looked amazing.

All of a sudden, we're surrounded and they're hurling snowballs at us.

"No humping eighth graders in my front yard," Spencer says.

Billy Ray jumps up, tackles Spencer, and presses his face into the snow. "I'm not humping anybody!"

Billy Ray comes back over, helps me up, and congratulates me on my touchdown. Then he starts apologizing. I tell him it's okay, we're just playing football. I say good-bye to Lucinda and then give Spencer and the rest of the dumb-asses the evil eye. Billy Ray and I walk home in silence. The snow keeps falling. I cock my head back, stick out my tongue, and feel the flakes melt as they land. People talk about falling in love at first sight. That's never happened to me, but a few minutes ago, I think I fell in love at first touch. I feel like I'm being swirled around in a velvety golden spiral.

When we get to my house, I say, "Want some hot cocoa?"

"I'd love some, but I'm too dirty to go inside," he says.

"I'll bring it out here. It won't take but a minute or two."

I rush inside and find Mama and the twins watching Joey the Clown on TV. They don't pay me any attention and I'm thrilled. I turn on the stove, heat the milk in a pan, and then add plenty of Hershey's chocolate syrup. Then I pour the steaming liquid into two blue mugs, plop a couple of marshmallows into each, and take them outside.

Billy Ray is sitting in the porch swing. He gets up and closes the door, then takes a cup for himself. We sit in the swing with our hot chocolate. His thigh is up against mine. I can hear his breath. I feel steamy inside, and it's not from the warm drink. After a while I let my head fall onto his shoulder and he puts his arm around the back of the swing. We take tiny sips of the sweet, dark milk and watch the snowflakes float by like tiny white butterflies.

20

neur·as·the·nia

*1: nervous exhaustion due to overwrought
thoughts and emotions
2: a neurosis accompanied by various aches and pains with
no discernible organic cause and characterized by extreme
mental and physical fatigue*

Jittery as a baby June bug, that's how I feel as I sit at the
kitchen table studying the "Tt" chapter of the dictionary. I
feel worn-out, like I've been flying too high for too long, with
no place to land. I lost miles of sleep worrying about the state
spelling bee. It feels good to be the center of attention, but it
also makes me feel creepy, like I'm some kind of fake prophet.
Mama says my ability to spell is a gift that has to be respected
because it comes from the Lord God Almighty. That sounds
true enough, but I think I ought to get a little bit of credit for
studying my butt off.
I wish Mrs. Harrison would hurry up and get here.

Maybe a smoke will relax me. I pick up the new Dublin-
shaped Kaywoodie Mama's going to send to Daddy at
Winding Springs. I admire its dark brown, gleaming wood.
It cost two books of Green Stamps, which is the exact same
price as the Magnan Aristocrat tennis racket I admired in
the *Ideabook of Distinguished Merchandise* for months. If

Mama had bought the tennis racket instead of the pipe, I might be playing tennis over in Catawba Hills with some rich kid instead of sitting at the kitchen table trying to resist the temptation to smoke this shiny pipe.

I rip open the pouch of Prince Albert Cherry Tobacco. *Damn it all to hell.* The tobacco scatters all over the table and some falls onto the floor. I rake the tobacco into a pile and cram some of it into the pipe. Then I strike a match, hold it to the bowl, and suck hard until the tobacco catches on fire. Yukkety-yuk-yuk. The taste doesn't come close to the heavenly smell of cherries roasting.

Huffing and puffing, I flip through the "Tt" chapter. *Taciturn* means you are fond of silence. *Terrigenous* is a gorgeous-sounding word that means produced by the earth. *Testes* is the plural of *testis*, which is the Latin word for testicles. *Testis* originally meant witness, which makes sense, because a man's *testes* bear witness to his virility. *Truculent* rhymes with succulent, but means something brutal, harsh, or violent. I also learn that if my friend Jamie Ledbetter follows in his undertaker daddy's footsteps, he will be a *thanatologist* one day. But my biggest surprise is discovering that Mama's numero uno belief has a name: *teleology*. The doctrine that all things in nature have a purpose—they are made to fulfill a plan. My own personal interpretation of teleology is that there is a Big Something Out There that is the Cause of Everything.

Maybe it is just the words I happen to notice this morning, but "Tt" words seem a lot more profound than words beginning with other letters. When the pipe goes out, I empty and clean it real good before putting it away. Then I get rid of any incriminating evidence left on the table and floor. A car horn honks three times. I grab my cowboy hat and rush out the door to Mrs. Harrison's station wagon parked in the driveway. She opens the passenger door and I slip into the front seat.

"I really like that outfit. You look cute," she says as she backs the car out of the driveway. There isn't a trace of sarcasm in the compliment.

"Thank you," I say. "Mama can barely tolerate it."

She drives north on Highway 200 toward town.

My new western attire causes a lot of raised eyebrows, but I haven't told anyone that my sudden change in apparel springs straight from a dream. In the dream, I'm standing behind a fence, watching two white horses dancing in yellow light in a faraway field. They are majestic, like the King and Queen of Horses. They rear up on hind legs and prance in my direction, while I cringe, afraid their hooves will stomp me straight into heaven. But then they arrive, snorting horsefully, and stand there, as if they were waiting for me. Suddenly, I raise my huge head and stand on four strong legs, only to discover that I am not a girl, but a white horse just like them.

After dreaming about the horses for the third time, I decided to get suited up, just in case a noble steed gallops into my life. I purchased Wrangler jeans in the boys' department at Belk, then ordered a pair of red leather cowboy boots from the Sears catalogue with my babysitting money. The shiny sheriff's badge I bought at Harper's Dime Store for seventy-seven cents, and I borrowed two of Daddy's old western shirts, whittled them down, and sewed them up to fit me. After Wendell gave me an old cowboy hat his daddy used to wear before he died, the look was complete. Wendell Whetstone Sr. must have been a pinhead, because his hat fits me fine.

"Hey, it's that crazy song!" Mrs. Harrison turns up the volume on the radio. "MacArthur Park" is the most frustratingly beautiful song I have ever heard. That image of a cake being left out in the rain with all that sweet green icing flowing down breaks my heart. The fact that it's sung by that sad-eyed actor who plays King Arthur in *Camelot* makes it even more enigmatic.

We sing along with King Arthur about drinking warm wine, about passion flowing like a river through the sky, about things melting in the dark. When we get to the tragedy about losing the cake recipe, we scream the last lines—"Oh, no! Oh, no, no, no, oh, NO!—then laugh our butts off.

"Look, Karlene," Mrs. Harrison says as we drive past my church. The sign out front has a brand-new message: ONLY SIX MORE DAYS TO PRAY FOR KARLENE KAYE BRIDGES TO WIN THE NATIONAL SPELLING BEE.

"Preacher Smoot loves to embarrass me."

"Oh, come on. It's sweet."

"That's because they're not praying for Amanda Mathilda Harrison," I say.

"You got a point there." She's got that glad-to-be-alive look on her face.

When we pass the cab stand, I yell hey at Kelly, who's sitting on a stool carving a wolf out of a big cedar log. He waves at me. Mrs. Harrison parks the car in front of the Red Clover Drug Store. When we walk into the store, Mr. Higgins, the squatty gray-haired pharmacist, is standing in the back filling prescriptions while Mrs. Higgins makes a milk shake for a young man sitting at the lunch counter. We walk to the back of the store to the café and sit in the booth Mama and I always share.

"Excited about going to Washington?" Mrs. Harrison asks, raising her perfectly arched eyebrows.

"Scared is more like it."

"Well, you'll be happy to know, all the Avon Ladies in North Carolina are praying for you. At the statewide meeting last week, my mother asked them to."

"I appreciate it," I say.

Mrs. Higgins shuffles up to the table with her green apron wrapped around her tiny body and takes our order. Mrs. Harrison orders a ham salad sandwich. I feel a little queasy, but order a grilled pimento cheese anyway. We both order Cokes.

"You ready to do the interview for your final home ec project?" Mrs. Harrison says.

"Yes ma'am." I pull out my little spiral notepad and pencil.

Mrs. Higgins brings a tray holding two small bottles of Coke with straws sticking out of each them.

"What's your topic?" Mrs. Harrison says.

"I decided to do my essay on the psychological and spiritual aspects of homemaking."

She whistles through her front teeth. "Ooh-wee. That's quite a topic for a fourteen-year-old. Fire away," she says, amused to pieces.

"What is the key to your success as a wife and mother as well as your being a wonderful teacher?"

"Hmm. Well, the first thing I do when I get up in the morning is thank God I woke up. Then I try to set my mind on enjoying the things I have to do that day—even the things I don't want to do. Being cheerful goes a long way in this world."

The sandwich platters arrive, each with a fat dill pickle and two handfuls of potato chips on the side. I trade my potato chips for Mrs. Harrison's pickle. She takes a bite of her sandwich and I bite into a pickle.

"Mr. Harrison is always whistling and acting cheerful. Why is that?"

"Off the record?" she asks.

"Of course."

"It's because I give him all the sex the Good Lord will allow."

"What do you mean?" I ask, nibbling on the pen. I've never heard *sex* and *the Good Lord* in the same sentence.

"The summer before I left for college, my mother and I had some serious discussions. She told me I had been given a powerful tool and that I must learn to use it with every single ounce of my intelligence, including my brain and my heart.

She said sex was a privilege that God gave us not only for our pleasure, but for his, and that—"

"Whoa, stop right there. I need to catch up." I look at the words I've written so far: *Sex, powerful tool, intelligence, brain, heart, privilege, for God's pleasure.* "Is this part of being an Episcopalian—to have sex for God's sake?"

"No. Episcopalians aren't half as liberal as my mother." Mrs. Harrison takes another bite of her sandwich and eats a few chips.

I take a tiny bite of the pimento cheese, then eat the other half of the giant pickle. "Well, go on—what else did she say?"

"She said that as far as body parts were concerned, eyes are the most important. And that before I ever let a fellow unzip his pants in my presence for any reason, I should stare deep down into his eyes until I saw the truth in them. And that if I was staring into his eyes, he was probably staring into mine, and all the looking at each other was bound to create a lot more mystery, which would slow the whole shebang down."

I scribble *whole shebang*. "You mother sounds wise as hell."

"Yep, she is. My advice for you is to wait as long as you can before you let yourself fall in love. Because once you do, it's nearly impossible to remain a *virgo intacto*."

"*Virgo intacto* sounds like a disease to me." I laugh.

"I'm serious, Karlene. Ten years ago, Jack Harrison stormed into my life, and I haven't been the same since. It's been a blessing, mostly. I have two wonderful kids, a fancy house, a jazzy teaching job, and a husband who thrills me to the bone. But sometimes, being Mrs. Jack Harrison feels like a *sacrificium intellectus*."

"*Sacrificium intellectus?*"

"Sacrificing your intellect. I've always wanted to do something truly great, to paint a masterpiece, write songs, or be an actress, but I don't know if I ever will." Mrs. Harrison pauses, sucks hard on her straw, draining the rest of the soda, and looks at me the whole time like she's aggravated with me.

"Have I done something wrong?"

"No, Jelly Bean, you haven't done anything wrong." She lifts her bangs and points to her forehead. "See this little wrinkle on the bottom? That's where I keep my dreams for you tucked away."

"Dreams for me?" I say, then lower my head, feeling shy all of a sudden.

Her finger lifts my chin. "Here's the truth, honey. Life is a runaway train. If you don't want to be another dumb passenger, you got to put on the conductor's hat."

"You looked in a crystal ball or something?" I ask.

"No, I'm looking in your blue eyes. You're so intelligent, it's frightening. But your heart's so hungry, I worry that, once you get a crumb or two of affection, you might end up throwing away your intellect just to get another crumb—before you even get to figure out your *raison d'être*."

"What makes you think I'm like that?"

"Because I was just like you." She smiles. The dimple on

her right cheek is so deep, I want to crawl into it, but I just sit there chewing on a pickle, feeling adored.

Owl-faced Mr. Higgins walks up to the table. "Hello, ladies. Sandwiches okay?"

"Delicious," Mrs. Harrison says.

"Just fine, thank you," I say, hoping he'll go away, but he puts his hand on the back of the leather booth and leans toward me.

"Well, Miss Karlene, you going to bring the spotlight down on Red Clover next week by winning the National Spelling Bee?"

"*Volento Deo*," I say, winking at Mrs. Harrison.

"Volento what?"

"Volento Deo. That's Latin for 'God willing,'" I say, then sip my Coke.

"How about spelling *apothecary* for me?" he says.

Mrs. Harrison says in her joking voice, "Excuse me, my dear, kind sir, but Karlene's taking the day off from spelling—"

"That's okay, I don't mind," I say. "Apothecary. *A-p-o-t-h-e-c-a-r-y*."

Mr. Higgins grins and says, "Got one more for you. How about *prophylactic*?"

"Prophylactic. *P-r-o-p-h-y-l-a-c-t-i-c*." I spell it proudly. Serious spellers never snicker at any word. In 1937 a girl named Waneeta won the National Spelling Bee by spelling *promiscuous*.

"Excellent. Good luck next week," he says, and walks away.

"He's a strange little man," Mrs. Harrison says.

"Mr. Higgins can be a pain in the butt, but he has some great drug store words. Last week I had to spell *pharmaceutical* and *hemorrhoid*."

Mrs. Harrison laughs. "Let's get out of here." She pays the bill.

When we get outside, a small line has formed at the Midway Theater across the street. "Jack and I saw this movie a while back. It's melodramatic. Prepare to have your tears jerked." She hands me a small cellophane package of Kleenex.

I stuff the tissue into my shirt pocket. "Thanks for lunch, Mrs. Harrison. See you tomorrow."

"You sure you got a ride home?"

"Yep. Kelly will take me."

I cross the street and wait in line at the theater. Mrs. Harrison heads toward the Ballet Barn to pick up Celia. I try not to think about Mama, wearing her hairnet, working her butt off in Weave Room No. 9. But since Daddy's been at Winding Springs, Mama works every Saturday, because we need the money. Besides, she's walking on air, thinking about boarding that plane to Washington, D.C., on Monday.

Inside the theater, I politely elbow my way through the crowd to the concession stand, noticing nobody is wearing western clothes or cowboy boots. Not yet, anyway. In Red Clover, fads take a while to catch on.

Billy Ray is standing behind the concession stand wearing a goofy paper hat. Every job, I figure, has at least one humiliating aspect. Billy Ray's main job is projectionist, but when there's a big crowd, he helps with the concessions. "Help you, mademoiselle?" he says, looking happy to see me.

"I'll take a Coke, *s'il vous plait*." My stomach feels a little achy.

He hands me the Coke. I give him a quarter.

"I like your sheriff's outfit," he says as if he means it.

"I like your hat," I say as if I don't.

We stand there grinning at each other. Billy Ray's been coming over on Sunday afternoons to call out spelling words, and I help him practice his French.

"Come by and see me upstairs between movies," he says.

"Maybe I will. Maybe I won't." I figure it's best to keep a boy off balance.

I sit in the middle of the third row from the front. My cowboy boots stick to the gunky mixture of Pepsi, candy, and popcorn spilled on the floor over the years. The theater is crammed with children trying out their bad manners on one another, but when Tom and Jerry scamper across the screen, the mob shuts up. The stupid cartoon isn't funny anymore—I have seen it twenty times, at least. I turn around and squint at the projectionist booth above the balcony and see Billy Ray's shadow flickering on the wall.

The minute George Hamilton appears on the screen as Mr. Hank Williams, my heart feels squeezed. He is so handsome, it makes my eyes water. His lips are thin, not full and luscious like Ringo's, but he has a sad, sexy smile. And that little beauty mark above his lip—I want to rub my finger all over it.

Hank Williams tears through his life like a tornado ripping up a field of daisies. I want to holler *No, Hank* a hundred times at the sad mess he is making of his talent. Hank was way too famous for his own good: people pulling and tugging at him, adoring him, wanting him to sing just one more song, sign one more autograph. Seeing the tragedy of Hank's life makes me think that the best time to be famous is when you're dead. Compared to Hank Williams's, Daddy's drinking doesn't seem so terrible. At least he did his drinking in Red Clover, instead of gallivanting all over the country like Hank, who also started popping pain pills. Poor Hank Williams had an awful case of the can't-help-its.

George Hamilton plays the role perfectly. He looks hollow, as if he already knows his dark future. I feel like I am sitting in the backseat of that Cadillac convertible with Hank, my thigh rubbing against his. I accompany Hank on his wild journey straight into hell, mesmerized by his hopeless eyes and his twangy, heartbroken voice. By the end of the movie, I've soaked every tissue in the pack.

As soon as the Three Stooges movie starts, I feel restless as a caged monkey. My butt isn't made to sit through a double feature, so I get up and walk up the aisle. The lobby is empty except for the girl working the concession stand. Her back is turned, so I lift the threadbare red-velvet cord that hangs across the staircase and tiptoe up the stairs to the balcony, which is empty. I walk over to the projection room and knock gently on the door.

Billy Ray opens it and motions for me to come in. He lifts a reel of film out of a dented can and lays it on the table beside the projector. Then he removes some old movie magazines from the chair and I sit down. My knee is about six inches away from his. Billy Ray smells like popcorn popped in British Sterling. I want to chew him up.

"You nervous about the spelling bee next week?" he says, all thoughtful.

"Nervous? Who, me?"

"Yeah, you."

"I feel like I've been eating pinecones."

The room is hot and stuffy. I feel electricity flowing from his knee to mine. *Now would be a good time to be kissed* is the thought I try to transmit from my thumping heart into his thick Boy Scout's head. Billy Ray looks at me with tortured eyes, then flips a switch on the fan. I feel a hot jolt of power climbing up my spine, a delicious feeling that I can make him do things against his will if I set my mind to it.

"Got something on your cheek." I lean in close and rub an imaginary smudge off his left cheek.

Billy Ray's eyes widen and he sighs heavily. We stare at each other. Then he lifts my chin and kisses me gently on the lips once, then again—not so gently. His lips taste like bubble gum. He stops kissing me, stands up, and pulls me out of the chair. His breath is raggedy. His arms circle me, hugging me close. My nose snuggles against the smooth skin of his neck. I feel his Adam's apple move when he swallows, and I lick his clavicle once, then again. Moaning, he lifts my chin and sweetly nibbles my lips. Mercury shoots to the top of my thermometer. I pull away gently, feeling hot and jittery. *Sacrificium intellectus* flashes in neon letters in my head, which reminds me that I have a National Spelling Bee to win!

"I better get back. See you later," I force my lips to say.

"Uh, okay," he says with a look that says *Please don't go*.

By the time I get halfway down the stairs, my legs feel rubbery and the lower-right side of my stomach feels like a switchblade has been thrust into it. I've probably worried a hole in it. I stumble down the stairs and into the bathroom, which is empty. I look into the old mirror with lipstick scrawled across it. My face is the color of chalk dust. I splash water on it, and another sharp pain takes my breath away. Something inside me has busted loose. The room spins wildly, sucks me into a spiral. I slump to the gray linoleum floor.

The next thing I know, Kelly is lifting me from the bathroom floor and whisking me through the lobby doors held open by Billy Ray. Kelly's taxi sits idling in front of the theater. Billy Ray opens the door to the backseat and crawls in, then Kelly lifts me into the backseat and lays my head in Billy Ray's lap.

"It's going to be all right." Kelly squats outside the car door. "Your mama working?"

"Yeah."

"After I take you to the hospital, I'll pick her up." Kelly

gets into the driver's seat and slams the door.

Billy Ray has a v-shaped scar underneath his chin. I watch it move as he talks. "Don't worry, Karlene. Everything's going to be okay, I promise." Each word sounds chewed up by fear, as if he thinks his kiss made me sick. I feel comforted being so close to Billy Ray, but I also feel scared. An image of a deer crumpled in a muddy ditch lodges in my mind. I try to replace it with an image of myself riding my white dream horse, but I can't. A sharp pain comes from deep inside. I cry out for my mama. Billy Ray says, "Shh, shh."

At the hospital, I try to stay calm as I answer the doctor's questions, sitting up on the gurney. Finally, Kelly escorts Mama into the emergency room, and I burst into tears when I see the worried look on her face. Billy Ray greets her and says he and Kelly will be in the waiting room.

Mama walks up to me trying to smile, then puts her arm around my shoulders. "You feeling any better?"

I bite my lip and shake my head no, tears trickling down my face.

"Mrs. Bridges, we've got a real sick girl on our hands," the doctor says. "How has Karlene been feeling the last day or two?"

"She's been complaining about her stomach. I gave her some Pepto-Bismol. I thought it was just nerves because of the spelling bee. She's usually a big eater, but she hasn't been eating much the last couple days." Mama wrings her hands, but her voice has that everything's-going-to-be-all-right sound.

The doctor presses three, big fat fingers into the right side of my belly.

"That hurt much?"

"No," I say.

Then he presses harder and it hurts like hell. I grit my teeth and wince. I want to slap his stupid face. Instead, I vomit greenish-pinkish lumpy stuff all over his shiny brown shoes.

"Nurse!" the doctor yells.

The nurse rushes over, grabs a towel, and wipes his shoes and the floor.

"Swish this around in your mouth. Don't swallow it." The doctor hands me a cup of water, then places his hand across my forehead.

"What's wrong with her?" Mama asks.

"Well, she's got nausea, loss of appetite, a slight fever, and tenderness in her abdomen. Sounds like it could be appendicitis and . . ."

"Appendicitis," I say. "*A-p-p-e-n-d-i-c-i-t-i-s*."

He continues as if I weren't there. "We're going to watch her for another hour, and if things continue like this, we'll need to perform an appendectomy or . . ."

"Appendectomy. *A-p-p-e-n-d-e-c-t-o-m-y*. Appendectomy."

"Shh, honey, please," Mama says. Every ounce of color has drained from her face. "Operate? Isn't there anything else you can do?"

"I'm afraid not. When is the spelling bee?"

"It starts on Tuesday. Our flight is on Monday."

The doctor looks at me mercifully. "I'm sorry, Karlene. It doesn't look too good. I'll check back with you in a little while," he says, and leaves.

My heart pumps sludge. A thick, yellowy silence fills the room. I watch Mama's face as fear turns into disappointment. But she tousles my hair and says, "I need to make a phone call. You just lie here and rest," she says, and walks out of the room.

The happy tone in Mama's voice doesn't sound sincere, but it's a balm to my soul not to hear the black disappointment she must be feeling deep in her bones. I wonder if they'll let the King of Mothballs from Sumter go to the nation's capital to take my place. The thought of it makes me want to cut out my own appendix. I have never felt so picked on in my pathetic life. The words *terrigeneous* and *teleology* and *truculent* and *taciturn* taste bitter in my mouth. I wish I could spit them out into one worthwhile sentence. But most of all, I wish I could unplug myself from the Big Something Out There That Causes Every Damn Thing.

"Hey, how you feeling?" Billy Ray's standing beside my bed, holding a bud vase with a single pink rose.

I sit up and roll my neck. "Uh, I must have fallen asleep."

"Got something for you." He hands me the vase.

I hold the rose to my nose and sniff, but it has no smell.

"Your mama called Preacher Smoot and he's called together a prayer circle to handle the problem. Guess you better be expecting a miracle." He smiles like a true believer.

A huge burp rises up out of my stomach, then another and another. Tastes like vinegar and ashes.

"Excuse me," I say, embarrassed for the first time. Billy Ray's heard me burp a hundred times, but now that we've kissed, it seems disgusting.

"You okay?"

"Yeah. Will you get Dr. Bauknight for me? I need to talk to him—alone."

"Sure," Billy Ray says, and rushes from the room.

A couple minutes later Dr. Bauknight walks into the room. "You wanted to see me?"

"I thought of a few other things that might be causing the trouble."

"You mind telling me what they are?"

"This morning I had a headache and I took three BC powders."

"Why so many?"

"That's how many Daddy takes."

"That's way too much, but I still don't think that would cause these symptoms."

"Well—uh, I also smoked a couple pipefuls of cherry tobacco."

He squints his eyes, but says calmly, "Do you normally smoke a pipe?"

"It was my first time. The tobacco smelled so good, I thought I'd smoke a little bit to see if it would relax me."

"Anything else you forgot to tell me?"

"Besides the pimento-cheese sandwich, I had two whopper-size dill pickles for lunch."

"You had anything else to drink besides the soda?"

"I drank some coffee this morning."

"How much?"

"Two or three cups—I'm not sure."

Dr. Bauknight looks at me like I'm an ignoramus, then paces back and forth beside my bed. Finally, he stops and says, "Given this new information, there's a good chance you're having acute gastritis, but I still haven't ruled out appendicitis. Just try to get some rest. I'll check back with you in a little while." He turns to walk away.

"Dr. Bauknight, I need to ask you something, please."

"Okay, fire away."

"Do you have to tell my mother about the tobacco situation? It was a real stupid mistake. I promise I won't smoke again," I say, holding my hands in prayer position.

He looks at me for what seems like a long time. Finally, his frown melts. "Tell you what. If you promise not to wear that cowgirl outfit when you get to Washington, I'll promise not to mention the tobacco situation to your mother."

"You got yourself a deal," I say, and shake his giant slab of a hand.

21

ac·cli·mate
1: to habituate to a non-native climate

Early Monday afternoon, as our plane starts its descent, I look out the cute airplane window and see the Potomac River and the Pentagon, which sure enough is a pentagon. Mama sits beside me with her eyes closed, her lips moving in silent prayer. Suddenly, there's a horrible sound, as if gravity were sucking a hole in the bottom of the plane. "Our Father who art in heaven, hallowed be thy name," Mama prays.

Mrs. Harrison leans over from across the aisle. "It's okay, Mrs. Bridges, they're just lowering the landing gear."

"Thy Kingdom come, thy will be done . . ." Mama keeps on praying.

I shut my eyes, trying not to imagine this jet plane soaring straight into the ground like a goddamn missile. Everything is shaking and shivering for what seems like an eternity, and then *whumphf—whumphf*. I hope to God that's the landing wheels hitting the runway! We're slowing down so fast, the back of my head feels glued to the seat. If I was the puking kind, I'd be upchucking all over the place.

"Thank you, wounded Jesus," Mama says when we finally stop.

Mrs. Harrison pats Mama on the knee. "You okay, Mrs. Bridges?"

"Fine. Just fine. Do you mind calling me Lila?"

"Not at all, if you call me Amanda." My teacher winks at me.

"Okay, Amanda," Mama says in this new, certain kind of voice she's been using since Saturday night, when Preacher Smoot's prayer circle turned my appendicitis into gastritis.

The baggage claim area is jam-packed with people picking up all kinds of luggage and carting it away. I thought the Charlotte airport was something, but this one is like a big city. Restaurants. Gift shops. Candy shops. I bet it's at least four times the size of Red Clover. Mrs. Harrison finds a nice man in a blue uniform, who takes our suitcases outside and puts them in a taxi.

"Mayflower Hotel, please," Mrs. Harrison says as she and Mama slide into the backseat. I sit up front with the driver, who's halfway cute and wearing a nifty beret.

"Good afternoon, ladies," he says, inching the taxi forward, trying to get into another lane. A crowd of people stands on the sidewalk. Foreigners. Americans. Dressed-up little children holding hands with people who love them to pieces. A gray-haired man kissing a young girl hard on the lips. A United States Marine standing by himself with his eyes closed, his hands behind his back, rocking on his heels. All of them waiting for someone to pick them up and take them to a hotel or a fancy mansion or God knows where.

"You must be one of those spelling champions," the driver says, looking straight ahead.

"Why do you say that?" I ask.

He looks over at me, his brown eyes shining. "You look

kind of smart. I figure the lady with the black hair is your teacher. The other pretty lady must be your mom."

"You're quite perceptive," I say.

"Where you from—Georgia?" he asks.

"I'm from South Carolina."

"I bet you've never flown before," he says with a half smirk.

I look over my shoulder. Mama is showing Mrs. Harrison the tattered *White House Tour Guide* she ordered after watching Mrs. Kennedy give the tour on television. Mama is rhapsodizing about how Jackie Kennedy was a terrific First Lady and raised her kids right and all that jazz.

"I've flown lots of time," I say, flipping my hair. "My daddy takes me out in his helicopter all the time."

"Friggin' idiot." He honks the horn and zooms around a white Cadillac.

I can't believe I'm sitting here in this taxi watching all these cars crissing and crossing the streets of our nation's capital. I close my eyes and see *vincere est totum*—to win is everything. My main objective. And to act kind and decent and ladylike, no matter what. But deep down, I feel hollow as a whistle. That appendicitis scare about wore me out.

Mama and Mrs. Harrison are yakking about the week's schedule and what to wear for which event. I'm surprised by how well they are getting along. They're different as butterflies and zebras. Mrs. Harrison lets her hair bounce around, Mama's is sprayed stiff. Mrs. Harrison has a master's degree, Mama barely made it through the ninth grade. But in her dress-up clothes, Mama looks like a rich, fine lady.

One thing Mama and Mrs. Harrison both believe in is getting me educated.

"Amanda, do you mind being in charge this week? My nerves feel shredded," Mama says.

"Lila, I love being in charge. Just ask Karlene." Mrs. Harrison winks at me.

"Yep, you're a real dictator."

"Ladies, we're on Pennsylvania Avenue!" the driver says. "The White House is ahead on the right." We zip right by, getting only a glimpse of the huge green lawn and the gorgeous mansion. Mama wonders whether Mrs. Nixon has had the time to do any redecorating since they moved into the White House.

Four blocks away, the taxi pulls up to the Mayflower Hotel. We wait in line as other spellers climb out of taxis with their parents, their eyes anxious. I feel happy as hell to see all the spelling freaks. They don't appear to be fingernail gnawers like me. They look well dressed, well educated, and well loved. Most of them are traveling with their *paterfamilias*. Seeing them with their daddies makes my body feel like a flat tire with a couple nails in it. I try not to remember the cuss words Daddy says in his sleep or the way his socks smell like dead squirrels. I try hard not to think about him running around naked in the snow on the hospital grounds. I close my eyes and take a long, deep breath just like Mrs. Harrison taught me. I imagine myself as a little girl standing beside my daddy, watching him gently remove a hook from my very first catfish. I hold that image steady in my mind for a while, breathing in and out.

When I open my eyes, I find myself standing on the sidewalk in front of the hotel. Mama's standing beside me in her beige linen pantsuit and bone-colored pumps, with her head held high. Mrs. Harrison takes over, confident as a Roman senator, and we follow her inside. The lobby is gigantic. Sunlight splashes through tall windows onto fancy rugs covering marble floors. The smiling lady at the registration desk asks about our plane ride as if she really wants to know. A bellman helps us with our luggage. His name tag says FRANÇOIS. He's wearing a nifty burgundy suit with fancy gold *e-p-a-u-l-e-t-s* that make him look like he ought to be working for Napoléon instead of carting our stuff around. In the elevator his long elegant finger pushes number nine. François and Mrs. Harrison are talking in French. Everything he says to her sounds like he's asking to kiss her pink lips.

François gives us a tour of our attached suites and then gives Mrs. Harrison instructions on how everything works. Right before he leaves, he says, "Good luck, mademoiselle."

"*Merci*, monsieur," I say.

He smiles real big, showing his pale yellow teeth. As he heads out the door, Mrs. Harrison gives him a dollar. Then she closes the door and kicks off her shoes. "Karlene needs some rest, don't you think, Lila?"

Mama looks me up and down. "You look worn out, honey. Why don't you take a nap?"

"Yes ma'am." I'm happy to obey, for the first time in a long while.

Later that afternoon I open my eyes and see sunlight streaming through the window onto a bouquet of yellow roses in a crystal vase. Mama is sitting in a green cushiony chair, reading the book about the contestants in the spelling bee. The GOOD LUCK, KARLENE! banner signed by the students at Red Clover Junior High hangs on the wall above the mahogany dresser. I sit up and lean a pillow against the headboard.

"Karlene, honey." Mama jumps out of her chair and stands beside the bed. "How you feeling?"

"Like a whale swallowed me."

"I'll get a washcloth for your face." She goes into the bathroom.

Mrs. Harrison glides into our suite from her adjoining room. "Hello, Your Craziness," she says in her cheeriest voice.

"Hello, Your Saneness," I say, still feeling like a zombie.

Mama comes back and she and Mrs. Harrison stand there looking at me, their eyes full of concern. Memories spin in my head of puking and yelping, appendicitis and surgery, of airplanes almost crashing, of sexy-talking bellmen in fancy uniforms. "I'm so tired." Tears leak from my eyes.

Mrs. Harrison kneels beside the bed and holds my hand.

Mama moves my bangs to the side and dabs a wet washcloth on my face. "Shh, just go back to sleep, honey.

We'll wake you for supper." She tucks the soft blanket around my chin right before the whale swallows me again.

Later, Mama nudges me awake and I look around, wondering where I am.

Mrs. Harrison is sitting at the round table, which is covered in a white tablecloth. "Are you hungry?"

"I'm starving, but I need to pee." I shuffle into the room with pale green silk on the walls and huge fluffy towels on the racks. A basket sits on the marble counter, filled with small containers of lotion, shampoo, and mouthwash. I pee and then wash my face with a tiny bar of almond soap. My eyes look clear and blue and untroubled in the golden oval mirror. As I brush my teeth, those familiar words run through my mind: *Crest has been shown to be an effective decay-preventing dentifrice that can be of significant value when used in a conscientiously applied program of oral hygiene and regular professional care.* Why that dumb sentence got stuck in my brain, I'll never know. But the rhythm soothes me.

I sit at the table and Mama says the blessing: "God, take this food for the nourishment of our bodies, so that we may be better servants of thine. And please, dear Lord, help us represent ourselves in a way that is pleasing to you this week in our nation's capital. In Jesus' name I pray. Amen."

Room service is a delightful invention. I adore how the shiny silver domes cover up the food. I'm hungry as a piglet, but I force myself to chew one small bite at a time, savoring the taste and texture of the lasagna.

After supper I pick up the booklet and start reading about the week's activities. The National Spelling Bee is the field trip of all field trips, plus, every night there's a barbecue or ice cream party or social of some kind. They're going to cart us all over the place, to the monuments, the art museums, the Smithsonian, the National Zoo, and the White House. There's also a big banquet on Friday night. By then we'll all be relaxed and friendly, knowing we're all winners and all that jazz, no matter if we misspelled *leukemia* or *rapscallion* or *sassafras*.

Across the room, Mama and Mrs. Harrison are sitting in big comfy chairs. Mama's reading her Bible. Mrs. Harrison's reading *I'm OK—You're OK*, a new psychology book. I excuse myself to take a bath. I fill the tub with the hottest water I can stand, add two capfuls of Mama's Avon bubble bath, then slide into the tub and relax. This bathroom is twice as big as ours, and ten times nicer. The twins are probably taking their bath, popping each other in the face with their washcloths. I feel sorry for Gloria Jean, who moved back in this week to be in charge of the Amazing Bridges Boys, but at least she has a husband to kiss her all over when the lights are out.

After I finish my bath, I put on my new yellow shorty pajamas and then slip between the sheets of heaven.

"Good night, ladies." Mrs. Harrison arises gracefully in her turquoise kimono and tippy-toes to her room like a geisha.

"I see why you're so crazy about her." Mama pulls down

the covers and gets into the double bed across from mine. "I sure am glad she's with us."

"Me, too," I say, and then we both say good night.

For a while I lie in bed pointing my toes and flexing my ankles to get the knotty feeling out of my calves. I sense the whale swimming in the deep, black water around the bed, waiting to swallow me.

On Tuesday afternoon I get off the tour bus at the Lincoln Memorial with Tommy Ludinsky, my new friend from New Jersey, whose acne looks like he's been fertilizing it.

"I'm not lying," Tommy says, fiddling around with his dumb tape recorder. "Someone told me that *freedom* is misspelled on the memorial. Let's see if we can find it."

"Let's wait for Janine." We move away from the rush of other spellers.

Last night, at the Great American Get-Acquainted Barbecue, we were divided into categories according to who our favorite Beatle was. Tommy, Janine, and I were the only Ringo fans. The other seventy spellers were divided like you'd expect. Paul had twenty-nine fans, John had twenty-six, George had fifteen. The three of us hit it off and made a pact to stick together during the week. Janine is from Kansas City. She's fourteen like me and Tommy. She and Tommy were in the bee last year, which they said wasn't much fun, since Senator Kennedy was assassinated the night before the championship.

Janine bounces off the bus in her purple culottes and

walks over to us. "Oh, no, not that dumb tape recorder again." She groans. "Aren't you bored walking around interviewing us?"

"Ringo people are the opposite of boring." Tommy thrusts a miniature microphone in front of her lips.

Janine pushes it away. "How do you figure that?"

"Of all the people I have interviewed, you are the only person who chose Alaska over Hawaii as a vacation spot. And your friend here from South Carolina is the only person who refuses to be interviewed." Tommy holds the microphone in my face. I jerk it from his hand and stick it in his shirt pocket.

"I did not refuse! I told you I'd answer your silly questions—just, off the record."

"You're hilarious." Tommy laughs like a madman.

"I had a very good reason why I didn't want to be taped."

"Yeah, you're stubborn," Janine says.

"No, that's not it," I say.

"Well, why wouldn't you let me tape you?" Tommy asks.

"I figured you were taping my Dixie Darling accent to give to Eric from Nebraska, since he's so damn tickled about how funny I talk."

"Forget about him. He's an asshole," Tommy says.

"I believe Eric's got a crush on you," Janine says.

"Forget that! Come on, let's race to the top." I take off.

We race up all eighty-seven steps and then wander off in

different directions to look for the misspelling of *freedom*. The statue of President Lincoln is carved out of white Georgia marble and stands nineteen feet tall and weighs a hundred tons. Looking rock solid for all eternity, Honest Abe sits in his big chair, staring out at the National Monument.

Being in Washington, D.C., is amazing. It's the first time I've seen history with a capital *H*—all the statues of presidents and soldiers, the U. S. Constitution, and the tattered old flags in glass cases. Being here makes me appreciate history with a little *h*—makes me realize how important it is—whether it's short and sweet like my friendship with Tommy and Janine, or long and complicated like with my family.

Standing here, looking out from the Lincoln Memorial, I can feel the presence of all the people who've been here before me. I close my eyes and imagine Kelly standing out on that grassy lawn a few years back, with thousands of people, listening to Dr. King telling them about his Big Dream.

22

quin·tes·sence

1: the purest and most concentrated essence of a thing
2: the fifth and highest element that permeates all nature

"*Exacerbate*," Mrs. Harrison says, sitting across from me at the little dining table in our room. It's Thursday. High noon. Only twelve spellers remain out of seventy-three.

"Exacerbate. *E-x-a-c-e-r-b-a-t-e*. Exacerbate." I tear off a piece of the croissant and dip it in my coffee, feeling relieved that I sailed through yesterday's rounds like a breeze. I was extremely fortunate not to get *ametropia* or *coffinite*. This morning I was thrilled I didn't get *ingravescence* like the boy from North Carolina, who sobbed like his dog had died when the bell rang.

"*Genuflect*," Mrs. Harrison says, genuflecting.

"Genuflect. *G-e-n-u-f-l-e-c-t*. Genuflect."

"*Rectitudinous*," she says.

"May I have the definition, please?"

"It's the adjective form of *rectitude*, meaning honest, virtuous, righteous."

"*R-e-c-t-i-t-u-d-i-n-o-u-s*," I say.

She calls out, "*Obnubilate*."

"Will you use it in a sentence, please?"

"Karlene's mind was obnubilated after so much studying," she says.

"*O-b-n-u-b-i-l-a-t-e.*"

Mrs. Harrison stands up. "I'm going to call Jack. The next round starts in an hour." She goes into her suite and closes the door.

I pick up what's left of my croissant and bite tenderly into the soft, moist layers of pastry filled with what tastes like almonds, butter, and brown sugar ground together into a yummy paste. Mama's still splashing around in the bathtub. I walk over, open the door, and put my head inside the steamy room. "How's your headache?" I say.

"Still pounding," she says. "Mind getting me a couple more Bayer?"

I grab a couple aspirin from her cosmetic bag and give them to her with a glass of water. She's up to her neck in bubbles, leaning against the back of the tub, wearing a shower cap to keep her French twist in tip-top shape.

"I'm going to go stand on my head for a little while," I say.

"Sit down for a minute," she says, then takes the aspirin.

I plop down on the toilet seat.

"Karlene, I want to tell you how proud I am of you for studying so hard and how much I appreciate all your help around the house. It's been a long, hard year. You and your spelling are about the only things that have kept me going."

"Thank you, Mama. I appreciate everything you've ever done for me."

"Now you can go stand on your head." She smiles.

The carpet is so thick, I don't even need a pillow.

Squatting, I put my hands flat on the floor, place my head between them, and then thrust my body into the air. My eyes focus on the brass knob on the bottom dresser drawer. The fresh blood circulating in my brain feels nourishing. I feel a couple centuries younger. I don't know if it's because of that miraculous blessing Mama gave me, or if it's the ordinary miracle of standing on my head.

Ever since I can remember, I've been doing headstands, mostly out of boredom and when there's not enough room to do cartwheels. I didn't even know it was an ancient art until a few months ago, when Mrs. Harrison showed me an illustrated yoga book written by Swami Somebody. She said it might help with my shaky nerves, so I started reading the book, and discovered that the headstand is the King of Asanas. When practiced regularly, it improves intelligence, memory, and self-confidence and reduces nervousness, tension, fatigue, and fear. The headstand also stimulates the pituitary, pineal, thyroid, and parathyroid glands.

The nerve impulses to my cerebral cortex have slowed way down. I can tell because I have that dreamy, alert feeling. An image pops into my mind of me standing on the stage with a gracious smile, holding a trophy, doing that little silly wave like a prom queen. I clear my mind and, after a while, gently lower myself back to the floor. Mama's still splashing around in the tub, adding more hot water, trying to marinate her nerves.

I take the tarot cards out from under my mattress and kiss the top of the deck, close my eyes, and shuffle them gently, asking for insight. I pull one card and turn it over. *The Fool.* I used to hate this card. It reminded me of how everyone in the family was always telling me I didn't have a lick of common sense and that I had a foolish heart. But I've learned from *Tanya Marie's Enlightened Guide to Astrology and the Tarot* that the Fool doesn't mean dumb-ass like I first thought. A koan from the book pops into my head: *A fool is not brave, but has no fear.* Koans really give me brain cramps, but I love how they're paradoxical and can't be grasped by the intellect. I adore the Fool's wild yellow hair and fancy clothes, and how the figure looks as much like a girl as a boy. I believe it's a girl. She carries a white rose of faith in one hand; in the other she holds a small black box that has every answer in it. A gray, wolfy-looking animal is her guide, and leads her from one opening door to another as they streak across the universe.

A fool is not brave, but has no fear. Maybe it means that a fool needs to be neutral in the courage department. Maybe it means I shouldn't be afraid to lose—*or to win*—the spelling bee. I'm not afraid either way. Victory runs deep in my arteries.

I decide on a winning outfit. I put on my purple vest and stick the Fool card in my pocket. I pull out my new white cotton slacks and put them on. For good luck I put on my red cowgirl boots and tuck my pants inside them. I cram Daddy's purple rabbit's foot into my pocket and grab my SPELLER NO. 17 sign and place it around my neck. Someone knocks on the door and I open it.

"Hi, you ready to go to the torture chamber?" Janine asks. She's wearing the cutest pair of green overalls.

"Just a minute." I tell Mama I'm going on down with Janine, and she wishes me good luck. I rush over to Mrs. Harrison's room and let her know what I'm doing. She says for me to spell my heart out.

I hook my arm through Janine's and we walk down the hall and wait for the elevator. "I love your overalls."

"Thank you. Made them myself."

"I made this. It's reversible." I open my vest and show her it's red on the inside.

We get inside the elevator and it whooshes down to the fifth floor and picks up Speller No. 51, a halfway cute boy with beaver teeth. His daddy's eyelids look like they've been propped up with toothpicks for weeks. Janine and I say good morning. The daddy stands behind his son and starts giving him a neck massage. The boy shrugs his shoulders, but the man keeps massaging them as if he's a dumb robot. Through gritted teeth the boy says, "Please—stop—now." The father removes his hands and holds them behind his back.

On the next floor the six-foot-tall redheaded girl from Georgia gets on and smiles at us, while trying to hide her shiny braces. The elevator opens onto the lobby floor, which is crowded with spellers and their families. Reporters and photographers mill around, asking questions and taking pictures. The crowd starts disappearing into the large ballroom down the hall. My heart is racing. My hands are sweating. My feet feel itchy. If I had time, I'd go turn some cartwheels.

"Let's go find our places on the stage," Janine says, and grabs my hand.

I tell her to go ahead, I need to do a nerve-check first. She pulls her grandmother's heirloom brooch out of her pocket and asks me if I brought my rabbit's foot. I pull out my rabbit's foot and say, "May the luckiest person win!"

She wishes me good luck and walks away. I look at the watch Mrs. Harrison gave me to keep myself synchronized with the schedule. It's a Timex with a groovy white leather band. Twelve minutes to go.

Outside, I walk on a pretty pebbled path on the hotel grounds. The sun is shining and the air feels light and perfect to breathe. I breathe in slowly and deeply, then empty my lungs completely. When it's done right, breathing is an amazing thing. I read about a group of people called Breatharians, who get all the nutrition they need from the air. Somehow, they convert breath into energy that provides the necessary nutrition. They drink water and all, but aren't bothered with having to chew food and digest it. Maybe one day I'll try that approach. I breathe in slowly, deeply, and hold it for fifteen seconds, then exhale slowly and deeply until my lungs are empty. This air is delicious in Washington, D.C. My head is totally clear.

As I walk into the room, I see Mama and Mrs. Harrison standing over on the other side, looking anxious. When they see me, they wave. I wave back and clomp to the stage, taking my seat in the second row of chairs. I am the last speller to be seated. I breathe in and breathe out. My blood feels bubbly and oxygenated. My ears are perked up to hear silent consonants and tricky vowels. The announcer talks about the agenda and the rules, and then introduces the moderator again, who's as handsome as Mr. Harrison. His hair is thick and black and wavy. Plus, he has real sparkly eyes.

Reggie Somebody-eski, a fourteen-year-old boy from Minnesota, goes to the microphone. The moderator pronounces the first word: *spatiotemporal*. Reggie asks for a definition. *Belonging to both space and time.* He spells it *s-p-a-t-e-o-t-e-m-p-o-r-a-l.* The bell sounds and the moderator spells it correctly. Reggie hangs his head and walks from the stage.

I breathe deeply, feeling lucky as hell not to be Reggie. Another speller stands, spells *tylosis*. The next speller, Missy from Oregon, misspells *usucaption* and walks off the stage. Janine stands erect and proud, clutching her dead grandma's cameo. The moderator says, "Pococurante." Janine crunches her shoulders up to her ears. "Will you repeat the word, please?"

"Pococurante."

"P-o-c—" She stops, then starts over. *"P-o-c-o-c-c-u-r-a-n-t-y,"* she says, with a question mark at the end.

"Oh, no," Janine's mother blurts out from the front row, looking all pop-eyed. The bell sounds and the moderator spells the word correctly. Janine smiles bravely and tiptoes off the stage in her pink baby-doll shoes.

Next, *commentatorial* is misspelled. Suddenly, my bladder grabs my attention, but I practice conscious breathing and it seems better. Tommy Ludinsky spells *gummiferous* correctly, flexes his right bicep before returning to his seat. The next two contestants misspell *cauterant* and *uterectomy*.

Holy moly. It's my turn. I walk to the microphone. I breathe in and out. My legs feel strong, my boots rooted to the floor.

"*For-ti-tud-e-nus.*" The moderator pronounces each syllable.

I close my eyes, roll the sounds around on my mind's tongue. I see the Latin word *fortitudo.* "May I hear the word used in a sentence, please?"

"The soldier was fortitudinous in the face of immense danger."

I breathe in and breathe out, then say, "*F-o-r-t-i-t-u-d-i-n-o-u-s.*"

The bell does not ring. *Thank you, wounded Jesus.* I walk back to my chair, sit down, and wiggle my toes in my boots. The urge to pee comes back. I squeeze my thighs tighter together.

The cute shaggy-haired boy from Phoenix gets the word *selachoid.* He misspells it, then shuffles off the stage in his squeaky tan loafers. The girl from Biloxi misspells *microstomatous*, after learning that it means having an extremely small mouth. I'm not nearly as nervous as I was at the South Carolina bee. This breathing in and breathing out really relaxes my frilly nerves.

All of a sudden, I get that weird feeling that somebody is staring at me. I look around the room until I see a man sitting in an aisle seat in the fourth row. His hat is cocked down on his head so low I can't see his eyes, but he has pretty teeth like Daddy's and he's smiling at me. The skin on my scalp gets the prickles. Now is not the time to get sidetracked on whether my daddy miraculously transported himself all the way from Winding Springs, so I force myself to turn my attention back to the spelling bee.

Veronica from Iowa steps to the microphone with a calm face, her bladder obviously empty.

"*Verisimilitude*," the moderator says, his voice as smooth and fizzy as an ice cream float.

"May I have the definition, please?" Veronica asks.

"Having the appearance of truth," the moderator says.

Veronica begins to spell. "*V-e-r-i—*" Then she stops.

Six-syllable words can be very tough, especially verisimilitude, with those four short i syllables right there together like that.

"*V-e-r-i-s-i-m-i—*," she says, and then genuflects before spelling the rest of the word correctly.

"Ladies and gentlemen," the moderator says, "we are entering the final round. Our three finalists are Tommy Ludinsky, from Trenton, New Jersey; Karlene Bridges, from Red Clover, South Carolina; and Veronica Baker, from Iowa City, Iowa."

The audience claps enthusiastically. My bladder is nearly stretched beyond its limits. I imagine pee running down my legs into my boots.

"Now, Mr. Ludinsky, will you please step forward?" the moderator says.

Tommy walks to the microphone.

"Fabaitious," the moderator says.

Tommy lifts his head and stares at the ceiling as if the word might appear. After what seems like forever, the moderator says, "Mr. Ludinsky?"

"Uh, excuse me. May I have the definition, please?"

"Having the nature of a bean; like a bean."

Tommy pushes his hands deep into his pockets, rises on his toes, and rocks back down. He pronounces the word, then says, *"F-a-b-a-i-t-o-u-s?"*

The bell rings and the moderator spells the word correctly. Tommy walks down and sits beside his daddy, stretching his legs out like a cowboy. My eyes wander over to the mystery man's chair. His hat is off now. He is not one bit handsome. It is definitely not Daddy.

Veronica walks to the microphone in her expensive white sandals. The moderator rolls his thick neck and pronounces, *"Lachrymosity."*

"May I have the definition, please?" Veronica's big toe flicks up and down, then starts wrestling the toe beside it.

"Tearfulness," the moderator says.

"L-a-c-h-r-y-m-o-s-i-t-y." Veronica steps aside, knowing she's right.

I sit in my chair, breathing in, breathing out, transfixed by the grand chandelier hanging above the audience. My whole being is focused on that single crystal tear hanging at the bottom.

"Miss Bridges?"

"Uh, I'm sorry," I say when I get to the microphone. "I really, really need to go to the bathroom. May I?"

The crowd teeters and giggles. The officials whisper among themselves, and then the moderator announces, "You have five minutes, Miss Bridges. If you have to take more than that, you will be disqualified."

"Thank you." I proceed off the stage with my head held high.

A few people snicker as I pass them. Dumb-asses. The bathroom is empty, so I rush into a stall and pee like a racehorse. Then I splash cold water on my face and wink at the girl in the fancy mirror while drying our face with a fluffy white hand towel.

Give me victory or give me death, I chant to myself as I march back into the room and take my place in front of the microphone. "Thank you so much for your patience."

"You're welcome. Will you please spell _____?" The moderator says a word that sounds like clave-us-in-ist.

"May I have the definition, please?"

"Harpsichordist," he replies.

Holy damn moly. "Will you please repeat the word?" I ask, looking over at Mama and Mrs. Harrison.

He pronounces it again and I spell it like it sounds: "*C-l-a-v-u-s-i-n-i-s-t.*"

The bell rings. Mama falls on her knees in the aisle. Mrs. Harrison wraps her arms around herself and hugs hard.

"Veronica, will you please come to the microphone?" the moderator says.

Ever so slowly, Veronica walks to the microphone.

"Will you please spell clave-us-in-ist?"

Veronica pronounces it, and then spells *"C-l-a-v-u-c-i-n-i-s-t."*

The bell rings. Thanks be to God.

The moderator spells the word correctly and says, "Miss Bridges, will you please spell rectilineal?"

Neon letters flash in my mind and I say them: *"R-e-c-t-i-l-i-n-e-a-l."*

No bell, so I step aside.

Veronica steps up and the moderator pronounces a word. *"E-clee-zee-ul."*

"May I have the definition, please?" Veronica sounds like she's been alive for two hundred years.

"Of or pertaining to the church."

She spells *e-c-c-l-e-i-s-h-a-l* in a dull, monotone voice.

The bell rings. Veronica steps aside, humming to herself.

I crack the knuckle of my right middle finger, and then spell the word *e-c-c-l-e-s-i-a-l.*

"That is correct. Now, will you please spell *surreptitiousness?*"

I close my eyes and pronounce it silently, sounding out all five syllables. "May I have the definition, please?" My eyes are still closed.

The moderator says, "An act done in stealth or secrecy."

I open my eyes and breathe deeply, mesmerized by the

huge shimmering chandelier hanging above the audience. But then my eyes focus on that one brilliant low-hanging crystal tear until I melt into it. I look out through its magic glass at the glittering facets of the girl standing on the stage, whose smile grows broader and whose voice grows louder with each letter she says: *"S-u-r-r-e-p-t-i-t-i-o-u-s-n-e-s-s."*

The ballroom explodes with applause. Flashbulbs burst, their light bounces off the crystal being I have become. The moderator pronounces Karlene Bridges, the girl on the stage, as the National Spelling Champion. Mama and Mrs. Harrison hug each other like long-lost sisters. A hundred cherry bombs burst me out of the crystal tear. My hands reach high above, and then they touch the floor. My body twirls through the air as if I am weightless. One cartwheel, then another—and another, and then I set my lucky red boots down on the stage. And with a happy flourish of my hand, I bow completely, and then lift my head, grinning like a fool who just swallowed a rainbow.

23

in·dig·e·nous

1: native

2: innate; inborn

3: having originated in, or occurring naturally in a particular place

Saturday afternoon, I'm sitting beside Mama in the backseat of Mr. Harrison's Cadillac, pretending to be asleep. Thank God, we're almost home. All this yakkety-yak about the experience makes me feel like a chewed-up bone. Mama is pontificating about the White House. Something about curtains. Yesterday, after we got our private tour, she beamed for hours. We didn't get to meet President Nixon and the First Lady because they're in Southeast Asia, but the White House was spectacular. It didn't have a family atmosphere at all, though, which surprised me; but the Nixons just moved in a few months ago, and they probably haven't gotten around to making it into a home. The Oval Office was huge and magnificent, but it felt empty to me, as if all the history had been sucked out of it. Plus, I kept having visions of John-John and Caroline and Jackie horsing around with President Kennedy, which gave me goose bumps.

"Here, let me show you," Mama says.

I sneak a sideways peek as she pulls out her tattered

White House Tour Guide and opens it to a photo of President Kennedy sitting in the Oval Office. She hands the booklet to Mrs. Harrison in the front seat. "Look at those gorgeous curtains Jackie put up for the President. They're made out of some kind of thick velvet material and fit the windows perfectly. Those flimsy things Mrs. Nixon put up look like they're made out of fiberglass and came straight from the Sears catalogue."

Mrs. Harrison shows Mr. Harrison the picture and he glances back at Mama. "You have quite an eye for detail, Mrs. Bridges."

"Honey, you don't know the half of it." Mrs. Harrison bursts out laughing.

Mama laughs along for a few seconds, and then says, "I know it might sound silly, but curtains make all the difference in the world."

Mrs. Harrison hands the guide back to Mama. "Lila Bridges, you are one unusual lady." She winks at me. "And you've raised one wonderfully peculiar daughter. I can't recall a time I've enjoyed more."

"I appreciate everything you did to make it happen, Amanda," Mama says. "It was the best trip of my life." She gives me a nudge to speak up.

"Ditto," I say, closing my happy eyes. "Ditto, ditto, ditto."

As we drive into Red Clover, there's some kind of ruckus going on at the Shirley County Courthouse. Sounds like a pep rally. Mr. Harrison stops the car at the front of the courthouse, where a large banner is strung above the second-floor landing: HOME OF THE 1969 NATIONAL SPELLING CHAMPION. Mr. Harrison walks around, opens my door, and bows as if I'm Karlene the Majestic.

"Thank you, my dear, kind sir." I grin at him and step onto the sidewalk.

The Red Clover high school band members are standing in formation on the lawn. The band is playing one of those romping John Philip Sousa marches. A big crowd has gathered.

Mr. Barrineau, my principal, and Mayor Melton walk toward me looking like they're about to greet the Queen of Sheba. The principal congratulates me and Mayor Melton comes over in his John Wayne hat, puts his arm around my shoulder, and escorts me over to the circular courtyard. A reporter from Channel 9 holds the microphone in front of the mayor.

"Ladies and gentlemen, we come here today to welcome and congratulate Karlene Bridges, one of our outstanding young citizens, on becoming the National Spelling Champion." The audience claps and whistles. When the applause ends, the mayor says, "Karlene, on behalf of Red Clover, I proclaim today to be Karlene Bridges Day, and ask you to join us in a celebration of your victory." Then he places a bouquet of red roses in my arms, and a microphone is thrust within an inch of my lips.

I swallow the lump in my throat, take a deep breath, and say, "I deeply appreciate the kindness and support I have received from all of you. Thank you. Thank you. Thank you!" I bow deeply. The blood pounds against my temples. I rise quickly and the whole world spins. I see the twins and Gloria Jean and Wendell and feel their arms around me. Miss Sophia comes up next and squeezes the breath out of me like she's my long-lost fairy godmother. Preacher Smoot rushes over and about shakes my hand off.

A sparking clean Royal taxi pulls up to the curb and Kelly honks the horn three times. He steps out of the car, waves both arms above his head, and starts making his way through the crowd. He stops when he gets to Mama and the Harrisons over by the statue of a Confederate soldier, and the four of them stand there, talking like the best of friends.

"Hey, genius," familiar lips whisper, barely touching my earlobe.

Standing there in front of me is Billy Ray Jenkins, who smells like a fresh-picked apple I'd like to bite into this very minute. The thought of it makes me swoon.

"Hey, yourself," I say in a girly-girl voice.

He sees my lucky boots and grins at me as if he were looking at the cutest, most hilarious girl on Earth.

24

myth·o·poe·ia

1: the making of myths and legends

Rich Hill looks like a homier kind of town than Red Clover. Maybe it's the giant pink geraniums in window boxes along Main Street. Or maybe it's all the interesting-looking antique shops, or the ornate traffic lights on the street corners. Gloria Jean turns onto Myrtle Avenue, spots a small white Winding Springs sign, and parks her new baby blue Mustang in the nearly empty parking lot. She opens the trunk and Mama grabs the handle of the manly-looking goody basket we put together last night for Daddy.

The center is a one-story building that looks like it was painted white a long time ago but most of the paint has worn off, exposing the red bricks underneath. A tall aluminum building that looks like a gymnasium stands in a nice green field out back. As we walk to the front door, Mama oohs and aahs over the red, white, and blue petunias growing along the walkway. I did not expect such a perky place. We open the door, a bell tingles, and a voice calls out hello from behind the counter.

Mama says hello to the unknown voice. A handsome-looking woman pops up from behind the counter. She has curly black hair with a touch of gray in places. Huge silver hoops hang from her ears. "Good afternoon, ladies, welcome to Winding Springs."

"Good afternoon. We're glad to be here," Mama says.

"You wouldn't happen to be Mrs. Bridges, would you?"

"Yes, I am." Mama sounds delighted.

"Well, Mrs. Bridges, I've heard a lot about you. Your husband is one of my favorites. He is sharp as a tack. And you, you must be Gloria Jean, with that red hair."

Gloria Jean laughs. "Yes ma'am, that's me."

"I'm Maxine Dixon. Pleased to meet you all." She opens the door and comes out into the lobby. Almost six feet tall, with big, broad shoulders, she looks like a wrestler. "And you must be the spelling champ. Your daddy is always talking about Karlene this and Karlene that."

"Yes, ma'am, I am." My heart gets a cramp thinking about Daddy bragging on me.

"Ladies, come this way, I'll take you to the Twelve Steps Room." She opens the door and leads us down a hall to a big room with a few mismatched old sofas and chairs in various groupings.

"You're lucky to have the place to yourselves. Most of the patients got a day pass for the Fourth. But tonight you'll get to meet some of their family members at the Al-Anon meeting. There's also a special group for teenagers called Alateen." She hands me a pamphlet.

I thank her and read the catchy title to myself. *It's a Teenaged Affair: Some Problems the Children of Alcoholics Encounter, and How They Are Meeting Them.* All the words in the pamphlet are typed in red ink, as if it were the most important document I will ever read.

"Now, ladies, please find a comfortable spot, and I'll tell Mr. Bridges you're waiting." Maxine walks away, and Mama and Gloria Jean make their way over to the sofas and put Daddy's basket on the coffee table.

I walk to the center of the room and stand there for a minute, soaking up the atmosphere of the place. The July sun flows through the tall, skinny windows onto the shiny hardwood floor. A new coat of mint green paint covers the walls, but the fresh smell cannot cover up the fact that thousands of cigarettes have been smoked in this room. The place has a relaxed, hopeful feeling. Signs and posters cover the walls, and a tall metal shelf is filled with books. Over in the corner there is a Coca-Cola machine and a popcorn machine like they have in movie theaters. I look out the window and see a cute little patio with a table and chairs, and, beyond that, a horseshoe pit.

I walk to the end of the room, where a dozen chairs are arranged in a semicircle around a wooden podium with a chalkboard behind it. Written in bold yellow chalk is a quote by Emily Dickinson: *Narcotics cannot still the tooth that nibbles at the soul.* A large poster of the Twelve Steps of Alcoholics Anonymous hangs on one wall, the Twelve Traditions on another.

I have been reading up on this Twelve Steps business. I asked Kelly so many questions, he finally gave me my own copy of the AA "Big Book." Kelly's like a saint and an uncle.

This afternoon he and Billy Ray are taking the twins to the July Fourth celebration at the fairgrounds, so we can visit Daddy in peace and quiet.

I hear a muffled moaning sound and turn around.

Daddy is standing at the doorway, weeping as if God just died.

Mama rushes over and wraps her arms around his sobbing shoulders, soothing him. "It's all right, baby. It's all right." Then she breaks down and starts wailing too.

Gloria Jean rushes over to me and pulls me out the door to the patio. "Let's give them some time alone." We stand in silence under the hot sun. My throat aches from choking back years of tears. Until this moment, I have never understood how I came to even BE in this world. But those people in that room, that man and that woman, the ones hugging and boo-hooing like babies—they love each other to pieces. If I had not been here and seen it with my own two eyes, I might never have known that I came from all that love.

Gloria Jean ambles away with her head down, her shoulders shaking. I walk over to the nearest pit, where three horseshoes are stacked neatly on top of another in the ringer position. The other horseshoe is leaning against the stake. I pick it up and admire the U-shaped piece of metal in my hands. I remember the last time I played horseshoes with Daddy. It was a couple summers ago at the family reunion, and I beat the daylights out of him. He had been drinking that afternoon, but just enough to make him halfway delighted with everything.

I might as well get some practice. I fling the horseshoe sideways like a Frisbee, just to see what it will do. It doesn't go very far, and it torques my wrist to throw it that way. I throw another one and it lands five feet shy of the stake. The next one is a ringer. I'm glad I haven't lost my touch. I pitch the last one and it bangs the stake and goes sideways.

"Hey, Champ." Daddy is standing just outside the door, holding two Tootsie Roll Pops in his hand. "You want grape or cherry?"

I walk over to him. "I'll take the cherry." I yank it from him in a playful way, noticing his blue eyes are red from crying.

"Where's Gloria Jean?"

"Taking a walk. She'll be back soon."

He unwraps the grape one, puts it in his mouth, and sucks hard. "Mmm—mmm," he moans, then removes the glistening purple sucker and twirls it around in the air as if he's worshiping it. "Every tooth in my mouth done turned sweet on me since I quit drinking."

I nod toward the pit. "You want to pitch some shoes?"

"Of course I do." He pulls out the well-used rabbit's foot I sent him and dangles it in front of me. "You're not the only champ in the family. Your daddy is the new horseshoe champion of Winding Springs." He puts his arm around my shoulder and we mosey on over to the horseshoe pit and gather up the strays.

"Ladies first," he says.

I rub my hands together until they're blazing hot, then bend down and pick up my first horseshoe. Holding it against my chest, I stand perfectly still and take deep, delicious breaths. A whiff of gardenia dazzles me as the sun's golden fingers dig into my scalp. I close my eyes, feeling light and delicate as a pink lace handkerchief. I find myself floating in the air above Winding Springs.

Down below, I see a girl. Her dark-blond hair shimmers in the sunlight.

"I'm going to whip your butt," her daddy says.

"Don't count on it," the girl says.

Then she releases the horseshoe into the clear blue sky as easily as a prayer.

Glossary

ab·ste·mious·ness
1. voluntary restraint from the indulgence of an appetite or craving
2. habitual abstaining from intoxicating substances

ac·cli·mate
1. to habituate to a non-native climate

ame·lio·rate
to make better or more tolerable

bib·lio·the·ca
1. a collection of books

dis·equi·lib·ri·um
1. loss of stability: being out of balance
2. loss of emotional or intellectual poise

du·plic·i·tous
1. marked by deliberate deceptiveness
2. pretending one set of feelings and acting under the influence of another

es·ca·pade
1. an act of breaking loose from rules or restraint

2. an adventurous action that runs counter to approved conduct

3.

ex·ac·er·bate

1. to make worse (pain, disease, anger)

2. to make more violent or severe

in·dig·e·nous

1. native

2. innate; inborn

3. having originated in, or occurring naturally in a particular place

li·bi·do

1. sexual drive, sexual energy: DESIRE

2. vital impulse; the energy associated with instincts

3. emotional energy derived from primitive biological urges

4.

meg·a·lo·ma·nia

1. a. mania for great or grandiose performance

2. a delusional mental disorder that is marked by infantile feelings of personal omnipotence and grandeur

mu·nif·i·cent

1. very liberal in giving or bestowing: LAVISH

2. characterized by great liberality or generosity

myth·o·poe·ia
1. the making of myths and legends

ne·science
1. lack of knowledge or awareness: IGNORANCE

neur·as·the·nia
1. nervous exhaustion due to overwrought thoughts and emotions
2. a neurosis accompanied by various aches and pains with no discernible organic cause and characterized by extreme mental and physical fatigue

par·a·gon
1. a model of excellence or perfection
2. a perfect embodiment of a concept

per·snick·e·ty
1. fussy about small details
2. requiring great precision
3. FASTIDIOUS

pre·rog·a·tive
1. an exclusive or special right, power, or privilege

2. a special superiority of right or privilege

quin·tes·sence
1. the purest and most concentrated essence of a thing
2. the fifth and highest element that permeates all nature
3.

re·gur·gi·ta·tion
1. an act of regurgitating
2. the casting up of incompletely digested food
3.

spelldown
1. to defeat in a spelling bee
2. to puzzle out; comprehend by study

sty·gian
1. of or relating to the river Styx or the lower world
2. extremely dark, gloomy, or forbidding
3. infernal, hellish

syn·chro·nic·i·ty
1. a meaningful coincidence
2. the coincidental occurrence of events that seem related, but are not explained by conventional mechanisms of causality

thau·ma·tur·gy
1. the performance of miracles or magic

vul·ner·ary
1. of use in the healing of wounds
2. a medicine of this kind